NEW VISION
PUBLICATION
P R E S E N T S

Cooper

# Damaged

*The Diary of a Lost Soul*

A NOVEL BY

# LSD GONZALES

*This novel is a work of fiction. Any references to real people, events, establishments, or locales are intended only to give the fiction a sense of reality and authenticity. Other names, characters, and incidents occurring in the work are either the product of the author's imagination or are used fictitiously, as those fictionalized events and incidents that involve real persons. Any character that happens to share the name of a person who is an acquaintance of the author, past or present, is purely coincidental and is in no way intended to be an actual account involving that person.*

**ISBN:** (10) 0-9826772-3-5
**ISBN:** (13) 978-0-9826772-3-0
Cover design: www.mariondesigns.com
Inside layout: www.mariondesigns.com
Editors: Linda Williams

Damaged a novel/LSD Gonzales


NEW VISION
PUBLICATION

P.O. Box 2815
Stockbridge, GA 30281
www.newvisionpublication.com

First Printing October 2010
Printed in Canada


10   9   8   7   6   5   4   3   2   1

*For Rolanda Chung. You stood by me when no one else did. Your strength has kept me fighting. My love for you runs deep.*

# DEDICATION

This book is dedicated to my mother, Maria "Saro" Gonzalez, who departed this world on October 15, 2009. Mom, I love you like I never loved anyone before. R.I.P. I miss you and I promise I will be the man you always wanted me to be. I love you!

# ACKNOWLEDGMENTS

First I want to thank the Queen who made my dreams come true, Linda Williams. Words can't express my gratitude towards you. From day one, you have been schooling me. You have been a real friend, and you have kept it ONE HUNDRED with me. Please know that no matter which road this writing game takes me, I'm riding with you. **"DEATH BEFORE DISHONOR."**

Now to all the people who been by my side and believed in me: Zafir, Fred, Malik, Run Tommy, Ray-Ray, PHD. Rock, Chuck, Julia, Caz, Ike Damari, Tony Elisabeth, Jennifer, Julie, Tambo, Jacob, Ana Jay, Eva, Jenny, Pooh, Ray Yabor, Ray Pastrana and family, Roger, Julia Lopez, G.D. Ruben Dollar, Maria Hinogjosa and family, Frank Ross, John Griffin, Cool Ed, Dr. Jill M. Doezer. King Sun, all my NYC brothers—too many to mention—and to all the real people who had kept it one hundred with me. If I didn't mention you, don't blame me; blame it on my memory.

To all the brothers on lock down in the State and Federal systems, keep fighting; never give up. Only a weak man would stop believing in freedom. It's time to man up! Only you can make it happen for yourself.

A special shout out to all the writers who keep me reading and connected to the streets: Joy King, thanks for all the books.

You are one of my favorite writers. Mark Anthony, Nikki Turner, Wahida Clark and Jimmy DaSaint, you guys inspire me to write at my best.

Also to all my fan club of haters, good looking out, because none of you guys can f--- with me. Just keep hating until you die! I show love to those who earn it.

# PROLOGUE

"Ladies and gentlemen of the jury, I ask you to please do not let the defendant's baby face fool you. Yes, her story of abuse is heartfelt, but we are not here for that. This is not an abuse case- this is a manslaughter case. These are nothing but allegations. There is nothing on record to support her claims. However, the evidence shows that the defendant is a ruthless, vicious killer and deserves to be prosecuted to the fullest extent. The victims in this case deserve justice, and only you, ladies and gentlemen of this jury, can provide that justice."

*How the fuck can justice be served when there's not one black or Hispanic on the fucking jury? I can't believe this shit!* I thought to myself as the prosecutor kept running his fucking mouth.

"Ladies and gentlemen of the jury, take a look at the defendant. Her baby face still holds a sense of innocence, but her heart speaks murder. As a father, a brother and a servant of this community, I can no longer tolerate our youth running around this city acting if they were grown up. When do we, law-abiding citizens, put a stop to the madness that our youths are engaging in today? In my twenty years of service, I have never witnessed a case of such malice. Since when do kids go around murdering their parents simply because they don't want to follow the rules their parents put in place? Today, ladies and gentlemen of the jury, you have the opportunity to send all out of control youth in this city a clear message, that we, the people, will not tolerate any disrespect towards our parents. I'm asking you on behalf of the people of Philadelphia to do the right thing, and find the defendant guilty as charged."

It took the jury less then three hours to determine my fate. I glanced over at my lawyer. He appeared confident, as he had since the trial began.

The judge looked at me with a perverted smile. "Will the defendant please rise!" The judge addressed the jury foreman. "Has the jury reach a verdict?"

I smiled and began screaming at the jury. "You white muthafuckas can't wait to send me away! Fuck you all! I don't give a fuck! I rather be in jail than in this courtroom where you racist assholes wanna sit up there pretending like you know what happened. Fuck you! Fuck you!"

The spectators in the courtroom went bananas.

"Quiet! Quiet! Quiet in the courtroom!" the judge shouted, ordering the deputies to cuff me up immediately. "Young lady, one more outburst like that, and I swear I will charge you with--"

"Kiss my Puerto Rican ass, you white devil!"

"Jury foreman, please read the verdict," the judge ordered.

"Your Honor, we the jury find the defendant--"

"I don't give a fuck what you white muthafuckas think of me!" This shit was like a bad dream. I looked at the jury and shook my head in amazement. Twelve members of my community decided my fate, and not one had the courage to look at me... not one!

"Young lady--"

"Fuck you, Your Honor!"

"Can the foreman please read the verdict now!"

# Part One

# CHAPTER 1
## "Lost and Turned Out"

"Breathe, baby! Please, breathe! Now push! It's coming… push a little harder… push!" I heard the nurse say while she held my hand as I forced myself to give birth to a fucking child conceived due to my infidelity.

"Push, baby! Push, baby! Push! I can see the head!" the nurse said.

I squeezed my husband's hand tightly, but the damn pain! The fucking baby's head wouldn't come out! After seventeen hours of trying to spit the baby out, I passed out.

"We're losing her! We're losing her!" the nurse shouted as doctors rushed into the delivery room to attend to me.

Rafael stood by me without a worry in the world, watching me suffer the consequences of my infidelity. *Bitch, look at you now! Look at you, screaming and hollering. Is that how you screamed when you was fucking some other nigga? I hope the fucking baby dies!*

As I lay on the operating table, Rafael held my hand. This was supposed to be the happiest day of our lives, yet Rafael was too uptight. Deep down in his heart, I believed he knew he wasn't the father, but since he never expressed otherwise, I ran the okie-doke-you-gonna-be-a-daddy game down on him. The nigga wasn't moved by it.

"Prepare for an emergency C-section, now!" the head doctor said to the nurse who was holding my hand. "We're losing her, damnit! We're losing her!"

*Bitch, die! Die, bitch! I hate you! I hate you!* Rafael Mendez now was on his knees praying for my demise. *Payback is ma'fucka! I bet your ass won't cheat on me no more.*

The doctors performed an emergency C-section.

It's his fault! Yes, I blame him, 'cause if the nigga was handling his business at home, a bitch wouldn't have to seek some dick elsewhere. Niggas get all emotional when a bitch steps out on they dumb asses; on some *she cheated on me* bullshit. But they always want to mistreat a bitch. They get real comfortable with the pussy as if they got it on lock. Half of them ain't even who they claim to be. I mean, they floss their lil' cash and whip like they ballin'. They push a lil' weight on their block, and now they're gangsters. From time to time they might luck the fuck up and lock a fly bitch down, but trust me, once the cash flow stops, the pussy shop gets locked down, and a nigga must hit ghost.

You see, back in the days before I hooked up with Rafael, I was a fly lil' bitch. I was the bitch every nigga wanted to fuck, and the bitch that chickens, whores and hoodrats hated. My body was banging and my ass was fat and tight. I considered my ass my personal weapon of mass destruction. Any nigga who had been honored to taste this ass can verify this statement. My coochie was off the chain. It was fat and wet. My head game was special! I'm a swallowin' kind of chick, with no shame in my game. Once my jaw gets to lock on a nigga's hammer, trust me, he's coming off that paper.

In my hood, North Philadelphia, Erie Avenue, I'm known as a bona fide smute. I got introduced to the fuck game by an old head who busted my coochie open at the age of twelve. From that day on, my coochie's been on fire.

Then came "Captain-save-a-lil' ho", Rafael, a suave type kind of nigga. He was the neighborhood King Pin, and since I was the neighborhood Queen Bee, it was only right that he scooped me up and made me his fuck piece. Shit, why not? I was MVP in the head department, and his old ass was sprung from the get-go. You see, in my 'hood, old ass drug dealers always go after the young pussy for two reasons. One, 'cause a young chick is satisfied with just being seen with a drug dealer. And two, 'cause most of the time they could use these young chicks as mules to carry drugs or hold guns. Me, I was different, and Rafael found that out a lil' too late. I come from a generation of whores. I mastered the game from my mother, so by the time Rafael got some of this pussy; I was on top of my game.

Once Rafael came at me with his weak ass game, I broke him off with some head and a shot of young gut, and the same day I had the nigga eating out of the palm of my hand. I took his ass straight to the bank. The only problem was, Rafael had a lil' dick. The nigga's dick looked like it belonged to a six year old boy, but he made up for it in the eating pussy department. Nevertheless, a dime piece like me needs to feel some hard dick sliding up in my stomach every once in a while, so I was forced to find myself a nigga who could beat the pussy up raw. I kept Rafael on a leash. I had to. The stupid ma'fucka kept me fly in the latest gear, and didn't mind peeling me off with some crazy money.

My whorish ways is what got me in the situation I'm in today.

Mita Cruz took her first breath of air on Mother's Day, 1979. Immediately after she was delivered, Rafael took one look at her and developed an instant hatred toward the innocent child lying before his eyes. *Yeah, the lil' bitch is cute and all. Good hair, cat eyes, but she's not mine. No one in my family has cat eyes. I'm not claiming this one.*

"Sir, isn't she beautiful! Congratulations! Do you want to hold her?" one of the nurses asked Rafael as she slid a pink cap over the baby's head.

"Yeah, she's beautiful, but I'm not the father."

The nurse give him a strange look, trying to figure him out, because when he arrived at the hospital he'd introduced himself as Sonia's husband. "Oh, I'm sorry, I just thought--"

Before she could complete what she was about to say, Rafael interrupted her. "Don't worry, it happens all the time."

"Sir, since you're the only relative here, and since the mother is in a coma, do you want to cut the umbilical cord?"

Rafael thought about it for a long minute before he answered. "Yeah, sure, why not?" As he cut the cord, a tear slid from the corner of his eye. *Damn! If only she was mine.*

For the first two and a half weeks of her life, my daughter was branded Jane Doe with a tag on her lil' toe, 'cause Rafael was acting like an asshole. Since I was in a coma, there was no one to name her. Once I woke up, I was forced with the task of naming my child. Rafael outright refused to sign the Birth Certificate or give her his last name, so I gave her mine. What choice did I have?

Besides cutting the umbilical cord, Rafael had never held my daughter. *I'm not taking care of no other nigga's baby. Fuck that!*

"Rafael, don't you hear the baby crying? Can you at least see what's wrong with her?" I yelled at him while I sat in my filthy bathtub, rubbing my hand over my C-section scar and feeling ashamed, angry and upset 'cause I wasn't ready to take on the responsibilities of being a mother. Plus, I was undecided on who the father was. Lil' dick Rafael didn't have enough dick to touch the clit, let along create a child. The truth of the matter was, I had been out there slinging pussy like a crack dealer slinging crack behind Rafael's back to support my crack smoking addiction, which was taking over my existence. I got introduced to crack by Rafael, and soon after, I was sucking on the glass dick like my life depended on it.

Ever since Rafael had been forced out of the drug game, his ass stayed broke. The nigga went from 'hood rich to 'hood shit. The young boys ran his ass out of the game when they found out he was dropping dimes on other hustlers on the low. Instead of killing him, they took his package, his corner, and were now beating my pussy up, disrespecting his gangster. The nigga couldn't take care of me any longer, and these young niggas out here were more than honored to be able to fuck a dime piece; the wife of a has-been King Pin. I had to get my hustle on some way.

From day one, Rafael had been acting strange with Mita. I attributed his bitch-ass attitude to his not knowing how to handle a newborn child, but damn! It had been six months and he hadn't even held the child once.

"Bitch, you come out here and look after your baby! I'm not going to play *cabron* to no other nigga's baby!"

"What did you said, nigga?"

"You heard what I said! I'm not going to play *cabron* to another nigga's baby! You got a problem with that?"

"Nigga, please! You been a *cabron* before this child came into the picture!" I yelled at his ass. I hated it when he went on his lil' macho trips like he's still the shit. So to insult his already hurt ego, I added, "If you wasn't such a punk ass snitch and a lil' dick nigga, maybe you would still be the man! But no, the young boys took your heart."

"Don't let your mouth get you fucked up, Sonia! I'm telling you, shut the fuck up!"

"Fuck you, nigga! You ain't gonna do shit to me. Now go play *cabron* and check on the fucking baby."

*I can't hold this shit no more! This bitch is gonna feel all my pent-up pain today.* "I already told you I'm not looking after nobody else's baby. As far as I'm concerned, she can cry herself to death."

"What the fuck you mean, you not gonna look after no other nigga's baby? That's your daughter, asshole!" I was so infuriated that I had to put my crack pipe down and go see what was wrong with the baby. When I reached the crib, there was a big ass rat in the crib rubbing its tail across her lips. "Rafael, help me!" I screamed from the top of my lungs. Not that that mattered, because Rafael took his sweet ass time reaching the room.

"What the fuck is wrong with you, screaming like you crazy in my house?"

"There's a rat in the baby's crib!"

"Why the fuck you telling me? Get it out."

"I'm scared of rats!"

"Me too! Plus, that's your daughter, not mines," Rafael calmly said to me as he strolled out of the room, not giving a fuck if the rat bit the baby or not. How ironic that he hated rats, when he was the biggest rat in the 'hood.

"What the fuck you mean she's not your daughter? What the fuck you mean?" I yelled while I beat the rat with a shoe. I was tired of this nigga saying she was not his daughter. Fuck that! We gonna get this shit right today. I was determined to make Rafael check himself for his asshole ways. "Rafael! Rafael! What the fuck you mean she's not your daughter? I'm sick of you and your drunken ass ways. You always poppin' crazy shit out your mouth every day. She's as much your daughter as she is mine.

What you think, I fucked myself? Nigga, please!" I spat. I was mad. Mita with her screaming and shit had fucked my high up. She had been nothing but a blocker since she was born.

"She's not my daughter. You know it, and I know it, so stop you're fucking games."

"All you Puerto Rican niggas are the same. Always want to play supper macho. Take responsibilities, be a man, a real man and spend some time with your child instead of drinking all fucking day, and maybe, just maybe, one day somebody will love your broke, crack head, snitchin' ass!" I thought that putting him on a guilt trip would soften his heart. Not this time.

"Bitch, do I look stupid to you? Do I? Answer me!"

Rafael was standing over me while I sat asshole naked on the edge of the toilet. I wasn't gonna let this pussy ass nigga chump me. Nah! I got up from the toilet and popped him upside his head with my hand. "What's wrong with you?"

"What's wrong with me? You really want to know what's wrong with me? I'll tell you what's wrong with me, and maybe then you can fix it, *puta sucia* (dirty bitch)! You really want to know what's wrong with me?" Rafael helped himself to a handful of my hair and dragged my trifling ass back to the baby's room in front of the crib. Still holding me by the hair with his right hand, he snatched the baby out of the crib with his left hand. "This is what's wrong with me! This fucking piece of shit baby! This right here!" he screamed, holding the baby up to my face.

"What?"

"What my ass, bitch! You know what I should do with this

piece of shit here? I should dump her in the trash where she belongs! Bitch, you better talk to me now before I go crazy up in this fucking house! Talk to me, bitch!" The effect of crack and alcohol had Rafael tipsy, ready to do the unthinkable.

"I swear to God, *Papi*, she's your daughter! I swear, *Papi*."

"You still want to stand there and lie to my face, you dirty whore? I'ma show you I'm the wrong nigga you chose to fuck with!"

Rafael threw the baby back in the crib, dragged me out of the room by my hair, and threw me down the steps. Once in the living room, he snatched an extension cord from behind the sofa and started whipping my ass as if I was a runaway slave.

"Since you want to lie to my face, suffer the consequences!"

The extension cord cut into my skin, and with each lash my body went numb. When Rafael saw the extension cord wasn't doing any justice, the nigga started punching me in the face, knocking all my front teeth out, breaking my jaw and his knuckles in the process.

"How the fuck this is my daughter, when I can't make babies? Bitch, I'm sterile! How is she my daughter?" Rafael yelled as he walked out of the living room, leaving me in a puddle of my own blood.

I knew I was busted, and there was nothing I could do about it. *Damn! I didn't know this bum-ass nigga was sterile. Had I known that, I would've been more careful.*

I took my ass whipping like a true champ, but like the crack whore I am, it didn't matter that Rafael had just trashed the shit out of me in my own house, or that I had been the cause of my own fate. That shit never crossed my mind. As far as I was concerned, it was Mita who had been the cause of all my misery. From that day on, I was determined to torment my child. I got myself up from the floor and walked to Temple University Hospital and got my jaw wired up.

I won't front, the streets of North Philadelphia had a grip on my soul. I was lost and turned out, and so was Rafael. The nigga was now sucking dicks on the down-low to support his--I mean, *our* crack habits.

# CHAPTER 2
## "Stolen Innocence"

You heard my mother justify her trifling ass ways, and that shit sounded good. The truth of the matter is, mom duke wasn't much of a mother, and the bitch was a trick. She told her side of the story, now it's my turn. My name is Mita "Sweet Lips" Cruz, and I'm gonna tell this story like it's supposed to be told…

By the time I was five years old, I was a neglected child, and scarred for life. Even at that age, I knew my household was dysfunctional and not fit for the living conditions of any child. Yet, each day I reached out for the love of my parents, I got my ass beat like a cheap whore.

"Sonia, get this lil' monkey out of my sight before I kick her across the room!" I could remember him telling my mother every time I got close to him. The bastard would kick me and spit on me every time I grabbed his leg and asked him to pick me up. In his eyes I was fair game for his abuse 'cause I wasn't his daughter.

The more that the crack sucked Sonia into the gutter, the less she took care of me. I was practically taking care of myself. Once in a while our next door neighbor would feel sorry for my lil' ass and feed me, but for the most part, I survived off of powdered milk, and the free school lunches I got in school. Sometimes at home I would open a can of dog or cat food and tear it the fuck up. The dog food tasted like beef, and the cat food tasted just like tuna. At that age I couldn't tell the difference.

As the years stole my innocence, I became accustomed to being neglected on a daily basis. I knew that if I missed one day of school I probably wouldn't eat that day. By this time I had already mastered the art of thieving. No bullshit, life was rough, and it seemed like everyone else around me was doing just as bad.

El Bodegero de la Esquina, the storeowner from down the block, knew my situation at home, and used to let me help myself to whatever I wanted: Twinkies, cupcakes, sodas and chips. Like most kids in my neighborhood, we were the offspring of crack heads, and there were no consequences when one of the dirty old men in the neighborhood slid their hand down the panties of a lil' girl. Although I had the green light to take whatever I wanted, in my childish mind it never occurred to me that El Bodegero was looking at me with lust and desire. In his eyes, I was ready to be fucked. For a long while he had been taking a special interest in me, watching my every move like the Chinese do black people when they enter their stores.

*I can't wait to get my hand on that lil' cute thing. Goddamn!*

*She's a cute one.* El Bodegero observed me from behind the counter as I packed my backpack with all kinds of cupcakes, sodas, chips, Now-N-Laters, M&M's and Chicko-Sticks. I thought I was scot-free, when suddenly I felt a hand on my shoulder.

"What are you doing? What you got in your backpack? Let me see!" He held my lil' arm tightly as he inspected my backpack, pulling out the stolen items. "So you stealing, huh?"

"No! No! No! I'm just hungry. I wasn't stealing."

"Don't lie to me. Let's see what your mother has to say about this," El Bodegero said to me before I was able to spit out another lie.

"Please, don't tell *Mami!* Please don't! I won't do it again! Please don't tell *Mami!*"

A perverted smile came over his face as he eyed me from head to toe. He enjoyed watching lil' girls and boys plead for him not to tell their parents when he caught them stealing. It was part of his sick fantasy. "I'll tell you what. Come with me into my office so I can decide what I'm gonna do wit'chu. Let's go into my office."

"Okay." I followed El Bodegero with my head hanging low. I wasn't ashamed I got busted stealing. I was more afraid about the ass whipping my mother would put on me if she found out.

"I'll tell you what I'm gonna do. I'm not gonna tell your mama, okay? Come here and sit on my lap," El Bodegero said to me once we were inside his office.

He slid his dick back into his pants, then escorted me to the front of the store. "Do you care for anything else, sweetie? Help yourself."

The pervert didn't have to tell me twice. I filled my backpack with every kind of candy I could think of. I didn't even care that he had kept my panties as a souvenir.

"Come back and visit your *tio* tomorrow!" he yelled as I dragged my panty-less lil' ass home with a backpack full of goodies. I understood El Bodegero was a dirty old man, a social disease who by no means should be in the midst of children, and I resented the fact that I was the recipient of such a disgraceful act. But giving this old bastard a golden shower was the only way I was gonna eat that day. I was just a lil' girl caught in between the evil forces of a sick world.

As I sat in my filthy dirty house enjoying my goodies, I took my time examining each item carefully. Each candy bar, each bag of chips, each cupcake and each soda represented my loss of innocence.

"Mita! Mita! Mita!" My mother stormed into the house screaming from the top of her lungs. "Where the fuck are you?"

I wondered if El Bodegero snitched me out. I thought quickly and threw the backpack full of goodies in the closet under a pile of dirty clothes. "I'm coming down, Ma! I'm coming!" I responded with my stomach fluttering in pain. As I approached my mother, an acrid order arose, stunning my nose. Needless to say, my mother was a fucking hot mess.

"Why is the door open? And what took you so long?"

"I was doing my homework. I'm sorry. Please don't hit me!" My body tensed up as I prepared for my normal dose of an ass whipping.

"You're lucky *Mami* feels good today. But the next time I call you, your ass better jump and move quick. Now, go get *Mami* some water."

My mother always felt good on the first of the month. No trace of the beauty she once possessed was left. The bitch looked as bad as she smelled, which was like *mierda* (shit). She had scabs and blisters all over her lips. When she opened her mouth and exposed her grill, it looked like she had cancer of the mouth. Her hair was falling out in patches. Her skeleton looking body, which weighed ninety pounds gave the heifer the appearance of a bald headed monkey.

"Ma, here's your water." I handed her a cup--I mean a plastic soda bottle cut in half full of water. She snatched it from my hands, splashing water all over the place. Then she sat her smoked-out ass on the floor and filled her lungs up with crack smoke.

"Ma, why you always smoking drugs?" I knew it was the wrong shit to say the second it came out my mouth.

My mom just stared at me with evil eyes, slobbering all over herself. "This shit here makes me feel good; makes me forget about my problems. It's my "Doctor Feel Good."

"But it's bad--"

Before I was able to reluctantly finish what I was saying, she bitch-slapped the shit out of me, knocking me to the floor. "I told you about asking me bullshit ass questions and fucking up my high!" My mom was now standing over me looking down at me in disgust while chicken scratching her filthy ass. "I'm sick and tired of this loud mouth lil' bitch asking me stupid ass questions!" I heard her say in a voice filled with hatred.

# CHAPTER 3
## "Happy Fucking Birthday"

By my fourteenth birthday, I was developing into a lil' hot mama, with exotic looks and a fat ass that had niggas drooling. Young boys on the block were trying to pop the cherry, and nasty old men were willing to pay top dollar just to finger fuck my coochie. Having practically raised myself, I knew the street game like the back of my hand. I wasn't ready to spread my legs yet, but I had mastered the art of sucking, and the line of niggas was never short. Everyone in the 'hood has a hustle, and mine was eating raw dicks. No shame in my game. Mom wasn't playing her part, so I had to take care of myself.

I was tired of looking dirty, wearing the same old clothes to school and playing the background, so when my homegirl from school, Nancy, invited me to her house to watch porno flicks, I tagged along.

Nancy was half black and half Cuban, was my age, but she

was a lil' promiscuous bitch. At 5'3 and 100 pounds, girlfriend looked like she was seventeen. Her body was ridiculous. She was thick with a fat ass, big titties and a small waist. She had a chocolate complexion and the looks of an African goddess. Lil' mama was the center of attention wherever she went. Like always, she was hated on by the ugly bitches in school.

"Look! Look! Look!" Nancy said with excitement as the actress on the silver screen got down on her knees and started doing her thing, licking and sucking two big ass dicks at the same time.

I was a little shy to look because my sexual experience wasn't up to that point, and was limited to my imagination.

Nancy peeped my shyness and rolled her eyes at me. "Girl, let me find out you still a virgin!"

"I am. What's wrong with that?"

Nancy looked at me as if I was crazy. "You playing, right?"

"No. Ain't you a virgin?"

"Girl, please! I been fucking since I was ten! I love me some dick. I got to have it. Girl, you must be the last virgin in the 'hood. Everybody and their mothers are fucking. Cute as you is, niggas gonna be trying to pop that cherry soon." Nancy still couldn't believe I was still a virgin at thirteen.

"You really think I'm cute?"

"Girl, if you wasn't, you wouldn't be around me. I don't mess around with ugly bitches. You just need to get some better clothes, fix your hair up a lil', and trust me, mama, niggas will be fighting all over your ass."

From that day on, Nancy and I became attached to each other like sisters. We were inseparable. She let me borrow some of her clothes, and she became my teacher in the sex department.

"Look! That bitch can swallow a dick without a problem! Look! Look!" Nancy had me practice the art of sucking on a banana. After watching Heather Hunter's porno flicks over a hundred times, she and I thought I was ready for the real thing.

"Nancy, do you really think I'm ready?"

"Stop being a punk ass bitch! I'ma be next to you. Just do it exactly like you been practicing with the banana. Make sure to shape your lips like a heart, like I showed you. Trust me, that shit will drive a nigga crazy!

Blame was Nancy's half-cousin and her fuck buddy. He wasn't that fine, but he served the purpose. The nigga was a lame who sold weed for some other nigga, but didn't mind tricking his money away. Nancy had already given me the scoop on him.

"Listen, he loves young pussy. Trust me, he will pay. Let me handle this. Just do what you got to do."

I was just happy my best friend had so much confidence in me.

When we arrived at his crib down on Front Street, this clown was already waiting in his boxer shorts.

"Welcome, ladies!" Blame was beyond himself when he saw Nancy's ass hanging out of her skirt.

"What's up, Blame?"

"Nothing. Same old shit," he responded while looking me over.

"You like what you see? I told you my lil' girl was exclusive."

"Yeah, I see. How much this shit gonna cost me?"

"Just give me three hundred."

"For some brain?"

"Nigga, she's top of the line. She's worth it."

"Do I get a refund if she's not what you claim she is?"

"Alright."

"Let's see what shorty is working with."

Blame wasted no time in setting the tempo. Once we were in the living room, he sat down on a chair, butt ass naked with his hard dick pointing in the air. For a moment I was scared, doubting myself 'cause this nigga had the longest and fattest dick I've ever seen. He was packing at least 11 inches. I knelt in front of him and wrapped my lips around his dick like I had done with the banana, then took him for the ride of his life. At first when I felt his dick head knocking in the back of my throat I thought I would choke. I relaxed, and then visions of Heather Hunter sucking dicks in the porno flicks invaded my mind. I bobbed my head up and down, from side to side, until finally I had him deep in my mouth… so deep that it felt like he was touching my stomach. Slowly I slid my mouth all the way up to the head, letting my lips shape into a heart.

From the corner of my eyes I could see Nancy smiling. When she caught my eye, she winked. That was all the confirmation I needed to know that I was doing the right thing.

I tightened my lips and slid all the way down on his long dick. When my lips were touching his nuts, I loosened my lips a little and let my hot saliva drip down onto his balls. I sucked until my jaw started to hurt, but I was enjoying it. After thirty minutes of deep throating him, I felt him spurt what seemed like a gallon of hot cum into my stomach. When I pulled my lips from his dick, Blame was dizzy.

"Goddamn! Goddamn! That was the best brain job I ever had in my life! What's popping with the pussy?"

"Nah, nigga, She ain't doing no fucking. Only sucking."

"Who the fuck are you, her pimp?"

"Nigga, fuck you! You're lucky you got some head, you ungrateful bastard!"

"I'm only playing, sweetheart. But when your partner decides to drop those panties, I'm here. I want some of that pussy."

"I got you only if your paper is right, nigga," Nancy said.

Blame then drifted off to sleep on the couch.

"Damn, girl! You put that nigga to sleep!"

"My jaw hurts!"

"I told you he was big."

"Yeah, I know."

"You cool though?"

"I can't complain. I had fun."

"You ready to bounce?"

"Yeah."

"Let's roll. Hold up! Hold up!" Nancy said as she reached into Blame's pants pocket and pulled out a knot of money and peeled off five one hundred dollar bills. "He ain't gonna miss this."

Once we were back in her house, she broke the money down in half, four hundred dollars apiece.

"What am I supposed to do with money? I can't take this home. You know my mom be on some crackhead shit," I said. I was scared, 'cause I never in my life had that much money.

"I'll hold it for you. Tomorrow, we're going down Germantown Avenue, and we're going to buy your ass some new gear. You can leave your clothes here so your mom won't trip on you."

"I'm feeling that!"

"Now, I don't want you going around sucking a nigga's dick for free. If a nigga wants head, he got to come off that paper. Ain't nothing for free jumping off. Plus, you need a better name. Mita ain't cutting it. From now on, your name is Sweet Lips."

We both laughed our asses off. Nancy was my mentor, and I was her sidekick. After a while, everyone thought we were sisters. In reality, we were just two hot ass young chicks with no sense of direction.

On the day of my fourteenth birthday, I had planned to let Blame pop my cherry. Nancy kept telling me the bigger the dick, the better it was, 'cause then I'd be able to handle any dick. Needless to say, I was elated.

My dreamy thoughts of sex were interrupted when I heard a noise downstairs in the living room. Immediately I went into panic mode 'cause I knew mom dukes was about to start some dumb ass shit.

"Mita! Mita! Mita, are you home? Come down here and get your birthday gift!" my mother spat.

I lay in bed rolling my eyes from side to side and acting like I didn't hear her.

"Mita! Get your ungrateful ass down here now! I have a birthday gift for you!"

*A birthday gift huh? Yeah right! How the fuck she even remember my birthday, when all she does is suck on the devil's dick all day long?* I wanted to believe her for a minute, but that thought quickly disappeared.

"I'm not gonna call you again. I know you're up there."

I strolled down the stairs to see what this trifling crack whore wanted. Obviously she wasn't gonna shut the fuck up until she had my full attention. "Mom, I'm not trying to hear your dumb shit today!" I blurted out, looking her squarely in the eyes and wishing I was old enough to whip her ass.

"Since when you stared clapping your guns at me? What, you think you're old enough now? Is that what it is? See, I had a birthday gift for you, but now you get nothing. *Nada!* Nah! Nah! Fuck that! I'ma still give you your gift." She reached into her jacket pocket and pulled out a bag of dope and a vial of crack. "Happy fucking birthday! Pick one. They both get you high. You little bitch, you're never gonna be shit, so you might as well join the family tree, nah' mean?"

"Nah. I'm gonna be something in life beside a crack whore, dope addict, dirty bitch like you!" I yelled with tears rolling down my face. I strolled back into my room, crawled into my bed, rolled into a ball and cried myself to sleep.

At first I thought I was having a bad dream, but the shit was so real that it felt as if I was having an outer body experience. The laughter and loud noise were coming closer. I could hear them standing outside my door. The noise still wasn't loud enough to drown out the sound of my screams when I felt Rafael on top of me, ripping my panties off of my fragile body. I knew then that this wasn't a dream.

"I'm gonna teach you a lesson, you lil' bitch!" Rafael looked deep into my eyes while he rammed his lil' dick forward into my virgin pussy, taking my virginity with one stroke.

No matter how hard I tried to fight him, I couldn't get him off me. He felt so big and so strong. "*Mami* please help me! Help me, please! Don't let him do this to me! Please, help me! He's hurting me, *Mami*!" I begged my mother for help while she stood nearby grinning and enjoying Rafael's brutal attack on her only child. "Don't! *Mami*, please help me now!"

"A while ago you was clapping your gums at me. Now suffer the consequences! Don't worry, the first time always hurts. Afterwards, you'll get used to it. Plus, Rafael got a lil' dick!" my mother spat while wrapping her chapped up dirty lips around the devil's dick.

"Ahhh!" I screamed out in pain.

"Shhh! Be quiet or I'll break your ma'fucking jaw!" Rafael put his hand around my throat and squeezed hard, cutting my screams short.

"Daaammn! This pussy tight! I told you, Sonia, she was still a virgin. We could make a lot of money with this good pussy."

After twenty minutes of viciously raping me, Rafael busted his nut inside of me, looking into my eyes with a devious smile. He pumped into my pussy one last time, tilted his head to the side and whispered into my ear, "Happy fucking birthday!"

I lay in a puddle of blood and semen for hours. I still thought I was dreaming, but my sore, hurting pussy and the blood dripping down the crack of my ass told me otherwise. As bad as I wanted to be fucked, I never thought that being penetrated by a man could be this brutal. Losing my virginity to the man I once considered my father was insane. It left me mentally paralyzed.

For weeks after I was raped, I stayed locked in my room. I attempted suicide on a number of occasions by taking un-prescribed pills, and detergent mixed with gasoline, but every attempt failed. I wasn't prepared to face the world. I felt ashamed, cheap, dirty-- somewhat like my mother, something I vowed never to be. I felt so cheap that I didn't even want to face my best friend, Nancy. When she came around looking for me, I wouldn't answer the door. After a while she stopped coming around.

Then, the unthinkable occurred. As I lay in my bed plotting a way out of my misery, I heard a loud knock on my bedroom door.

*"Bang! Bang! Bang! Bang!"*

My tormented body began to shake.

"Open the fucking door now, Mita!" my mother yelled. When I opened the door, she slapped me hard in the mouth, busting my lip open. "What took you so long to open the door? You got one of them nappy headed niggas in here?" She forced her way into my room, checking to see if someone else was there with me.

I attempted to put my clothes on, but she grabbed my hand. "No need for that, baby. I need you to do *Mami* a big favor. I'm sick as hell. I need you to give El Bodegero a quick shot of pussy so I can get a fix. I can't do it 'cause my pussy is worn out."

"I'm--"

Before I was able to protest, Rafael walked into the bedroom and began choking the air out of me. "Listen here, you lil' bitch! You do as your mother says, or else!"

El Bodegero walked into my bedroom holding a bag of candy.

*Does this pervert think I'm still nine year's old?*

"I'm not gonna hurt you. Trust me," he said.

"As I said, be good to El Bodegero," Rafael said, squeezing my throat, letting me know what he would do to me if I disobeyed his orders.

Once El Bodegero was alone with me in the room, he wasted no time taking off his clothes. The sight of his large dick made me want to throw up. He was excited to notice how scared I was. It was a turn-on for him, the pinnacle of his fantasies. He'd been wanting to slide his dick in me ever since I'd peed on it when I was nine. The good thing about this nasty old pervert was that he was a preemie--a premature ejaculator. As soon as he ran up in me raw, he busted his nut. Nevertheless, the damage was done.

Trust is something I would never have in my life, nor would I ever trust another man.

# CHAPTER 4
## "Runaway Child"

After the stunt my mother and Rafael pulled on me with El Bodegero, I packed my shit and bounced. I had nowhere to go, no family, and very few friends. I haven't spoken to Nancy in months, so going to her house wasn't an option. For weeks I slept in abandoned houses. Other times I sacrificed my dignity by sucking a few dicks for cash. I was fast becoming a product of the streets, an image of my crack head-dope whore mother, and I hated it.

Tears escaped my eyes as I walked around Kensington Avenue looking for a place to crash for the night. Lucky for me, the soup kitchen at Kensington and Front was open. The director, a black lady in her late forties, took pity on me, giving me a hot meal and a place to stay.

Mrs. Penny had witnessed her share of runaway teens who prostituted themselves in the streets of North Philly. Experience had taught her that every teen had a different situation.

"I can't go home... I just can't!" I whispered as I felt Mrs. Penny's warm embrace. For the first time in my life someone was embracing me, not wanting anything in return. My tears flowed freely.

Once I had finished explaining my situation to her, Mrs.

Penny broke down and cried. "How can a mother do this to her own child?" she asked.

Mrs. Penny was a widow whose husband and son were both murdered in a botched robbery four years ago by a crackhead. Ever since then, she had dedicated her life to saving teens from falling into the pit of addiction. With the help of private donors, she was able to open Penny's Safe House for Runaway Teens in the same spot where her husband and son had been murdered.

Mrs. Penny treated me like a daughter, buying me new clothes and showing me how to cook, clean and maintain my hygiene. She also showed me how to be ladylike. The love and guidance that I never received from my own mother, she gave it to me.

"Mrs. Penny! Mrs. Penny!" I yelled. I was slumped over the toilet holding my stomach. "I think I may have food poison! I'm vomiting real bad! The pain is killing me!" Mrs. Penny picked me up from the bathroom floor and led me to my bed.

*Oh my God! Please say it ain't so! Please tell me this child ain't pregnant!* Mrs. Penny had seen many young girls in this same predicament before. "Don't worry, baby. I'm going to take care of you. Hold on, baby. I'm taking you to the hospital." Mrs. Penny threw a blanket over me and carried me to her car. I screamed the entire way to the hospital. The pain was unbearable.

Once we got to the emergency entrance, Mrs. Penny ran out of the car leaving the engine running, and rushed inside for help. Within seconds two nurses rushed out with a wheelchair and Mrs. Penny on their heels.

After what seemed like hours of waiting, a doctor came out and greeted Mrs. Penny. "Excuse me, Miss. My name is Doctor Glenn, and I'm the doctor overseeing the young lady you bought in here earlier. Are you related to her?"

"Yes, I'm her grandmother!" Mrs. Penny answered quickly.

"Well, madam, I have great news, and not so great news. The good news is that your granddaughter will be fine. She only had major cramps, which will go away once the medication takes effect. The not so great new is that she's four and a half months pregnant, and she has an STD… gonorrhea. I'll prescribe penicillin. Nowadays, we must keep a close eye on our children," Doctor Glenn blared out, and then added, "I want to see this child on a monthly basis. At such a young age she needs to be closely monitored. My nurse will give you a list of things to do, as well as a dietary chart, okay? Don't look so sad. My youngest surprised me with a grandson when she was sixteen years old."

"I hear you!"

"Good. Your granddaughter will be released in a few hours. She must take her penicillin twice a day."

The minute Doctor Glenn was out of sight; Mrs. Penny dropped to her knees and asked God for guidance. "I can't turn my back on this child!" she said to no one in particular. She turned her head to the side to hide her tears from the other people in the emergency room.

To say that I lost control when Mrs. Penny broke the news to me is an understatement. Now I understand why my pussy had been hurting and swollen for months. "What am I supposed to do? I can't have this baby! I'm too young!"

"You're too far into the pregnancy. They can't perform an abortion. Don't worry, baby, Mrs. Penny will support you."

"Easy for you to say!" I snapped.

"Just a minute, young lady! Whether you like it or not, I'm all you got right now. I love you like a daughter, so that means I'll stand by you 'til the end, if you want me to. Calm down. There's no need to catch a fit."

"I'm sorry, Mrs. Penny. I didn't mean to disrespect you."

"I know, baby. I know. I promise, I'll work things out one way or another."

"I'm scared, Mrs. Penny! I'm scared!"

Suddenly, I felt relaxed as if I'd handed over my drama to someone else.

An hour later, I was back home under Mrs. Penny's care, taking penicillin to cure my gonorrhea.

Mrs. Penny played her motherly role, but curiosity overcame her. She wanted to be a hundred percent sure that my revelation to her about what my mother had done to me was true and not some made up shit. "Mita, I hate to bring this topic up now…" Her face was flushed with embarrassment; possible anger, something she rarely displayed since the death of her husband and son. But she was damned if she was going to sit around and let a child rapist walk around her community.

"What?" I asked, offended that she would doubt me.

"Did your mother really make you have sex for crack money?" She burst into tears before I could answer. Mrs. Penny covered her face with her hands and cried quietly.

"Yes... yes she did. I can't believe it myself. If it wasn't for her, I wouldn't be pregnant right now. My stepfather raped me on my fourteenth birthday... took my virginity. A few weeks later my mother sold me out for crack money. El Bodegero raped me while my mother and stepfather watched. I hate her! I hate her! I really do!" I willed myself not to throw up. I closed my eyes as if I was trying to forget my past.

"Just relax, baby. Just relax."

# CHAPTER 5
## "A Ward of the State"

Four and a half months later, on September 13, 1990, I was rushed to Temple University's maternity ward. My water had broken while I was sitting with Mrs. Penny on her front steps.

The spirit that was felt when I gave birth to a beautiful eight and a half-pound baby was killed when a crackhead looking woman stumbled into the room, creating a scene.

"Excuse me, Miss! You're not allowed in here. I don't know if you're lost or not, but you must get out of here now!" Doctor Glenn said.

*"Smack!"*

The smack left everyone in the room in shock.

*Who the fuck is this sorry bitch?* I lifted my head up to see what the commotion was all about, and I almost jumped off the bed. It was like seeing a ghost. "Mom! What the fuck you doing here? Who invited you?" If I hadn't been lying on my back with my legs spread wide open, I would've beaten her ass all over the room.

"Mom! You're her mo--"

"Yes, I am, you asshole!" My mother slurred the words as she continued walking towards the nurse who was holding my baby girl. "And who the fuck are you?" she asked Mrs. Penny.

"I'm Mrs. Penny, the woman who's been taking care of *your daughter*!" Mrs. Penny made sure she emphasized the words "your daughter" while looking Sonia straight in her eyes. *I wish you would act stupid up in her, so I can whip your funky ass back to reality!*

Mrs. Penny was infuriated that Sonia was now popping up out of nowhere, wanting to claim her parental rights after she had allowed me to be raped, and sold out for crack money. On top of that, we hadn't even seen each other in almost nine months.

"My daughter is under age. As her legal guardian, my husband and I have decided to put the baby up for adoption. It's in the best interest of my child."

Sonia was fucking crazy. I lay in bed not believing what I was hearing. I didn't even get a chance to hold my daughter. I was hurt and emotionally fucked up. Sonia had found yet another way to hurt me.

History was repeating itself. My child was branded Jane Doe, just as I had been at birth. The only difference was, I went to an abusive mother, and my daughter became a ward of the state.

Snatching my baby from me was the proverbial straw that broke the camel's back. Sonia was the reason my life was turning out to be so fucked up. She had overstepped her welcome in my life. She had broken me beyond the breaking point. This shit was personal for me, and one way or another, the bitch had to pay.

*Damn! I'm hearing shit. I could swear I heard a voice. I must be tripping,* Sonia thought to herself as she lay back on the filthy couch in her raggedy house, which reeked like cat piss. She thought she was hallucinating, but she wasn't.

I was standing next to her filthy couch, staring down at her with pure hatred. "I can't stand the sight of you!"

"Oh shit! You scared the hell out of me! Bitch, didn't I tell you not to creep up on me? What the fuck you doing here? Let me guess. You miss me? No. That nappy-headed women you live with kicked your skank ass out and now you want to come back home. You're not welcome here anymore. Get out!" Sonia screamed.

"Mom, just tell me why? Why did you allow Rafael to rape me? Why?"

"Why! Why! Why! You really want to know why? 'Cause you ain't shit!" Sonia got up from the couch and was standing toe to toe with me and shaking her head from side to side. "As a matter of fact, if you want to be up in my house, you got to pay. Give me two dollars so I can get something to eat." She tried to put her hand in my jacket pocket. I wanted to punch her dead in the face, but I controlled myself, at least for the moment.

"You can't get shit from me but an ass whipping!" I snapped, and then punched her in the face over and over until my hands were swollen.

"You know, Mom, the whole time you used to beat me and abuse me, I thought of this day."

"Fuck you, you no good whore!" Sonia realized her life was about to end. The look on her face was one of desperation.

"Look at your trifling ass, wondering why the fuck I'm doing this to you! Ain't you curious, Mom?" I was on my knees, looking into her eyes. I wanted her to see my pain.

Once my hands got tired of beating her, I picked up an empty beer bottle and beat her in the face with it.

For a chicken head, Sonia was pretty strong. She took the vicious ass whipping I dealt her and was still popping mad shit out of her mouth. It was as if she wanted to prove to me that I couldn't break her. Her eyes told me she didn't want to give me the satisfaction of seeing her beg for her life, which sent me over the edge. "No matter what you do to me, I'm always going to be in your life! It's my DNA running through your blood, bitch!"

I couldn't stand the sound of her voice, so I started stabbing her in the face with the broken beer bottle. The first stab popped her right eye out of the socket. The second slashed her throat, and silenced her filthy mouth. After the fourth stab I stopped counting. *You can't hurt me no more! Never again!*

Then I heard the front door open and the voice of a man laughing. I ran towards him blinded with rage, with the broken beer bottle in hand.

"What the fuck's going on in here?" Rafael never saw it coming, never felt it, as I plunged the broken bottle directly into his heart.

*Die, you rapist!*

I sat on the front steps of the house, which had brought so much terror into my life, and waited for the police. The sound of sirens was getting closer. Neighbors gathered, trying to get a peek of the urban nightmare that had unfolded in their neighborhood. Suddenly, I got up, went back inside the house, stood over Sonia and Rafael's bodies and spit in their faces. *Go to hell, y'all bastards!*

As I sat in the back of the police car, I saw two black men in dark jumpsuits maneuvering a gurney. Suddenly, Sonia's body came crashing down the steps, like the piece of trash she was. I felt a hysterical laugh gurgle at the back of my throat. *I'd do it again if I had to.* At that moment, it felt like a heavy load had been lifted off of my shoulders.

# CHAPTER 6
## "The People v. Mita Cruz"

Nine months later, the Grand Jury returned an indictment against me for two counts of involuntary manslaughter. The District Attorney was prepared to fry my ass. Since my case had been splashed all over the local news stations, it was considered a high profile case, generating news media attention across the country.

I was being represented by a flamboyant attorney named Steven Perry, one of the hottest criminal defense attorneys in the City of Brotherly Love. His list of clients included rappers Beenie Segal, Cassady, T.O. and a host of other celebrities and corrupt politicians. Mr. Steven Perry volunteered to take my case pro-bono because of the publicity it had generated and the potential it had to increase his list of clients.

The mood in the courtroom was somber. The stage was set, and Steven Perry was ready to give his best performance ever. It has been said that to be a good criminal defense attorney, you must be a good actor. Believe me, Steven Perry would've put Brad Pitt out of business. His sense of confidence and control created just the right atmosphere in the courtroom. There was no denying who was in charge.

Jason Vega, a chubby faced Hispanic, looked over at the

defense table and realized he was outnumbered skills-wise. The only thing he had in his favor was the judge who been known to favor the District Attorney in most cases.

Once the jury was seated, the judge was prepared to move forward. He motioned to the District Attorney.

"Your Honor, this is the case of the People versus Mita Cruz, involving two counts of involuntary manslaughter. Ladies and gentleman of the jury, the People will prove beyond a reasonable doubt that on October 16, 1990, this young lady…" he paused for a few seconds, letting the jury get a good look at me as he pointed towards the defense table. "This innocent faced young lady decided to take justice into her own hands, and killed her parents simply because she didn't want to follow her mother's rules. The evidence will demonstrate that she planned and carried out these brutal crimes on her own. Don't be fooled by her tears and baby face. She's a murderer." He looked at the jury with a concerned face, as if he really gave a fuck about Sonia and Rafael, then sat his fat ass down.

"Good morning, ladies and gentleman of the jury. My name is Steven Perry. I'm here today because of extraordinary circumstances; circumstances no fourteen year old girl should ever experience. You heard Mr. Vega tell you how my client is a murderer and how she planned this whole ordeal. Ladies and gentlemen of the jury, there is only one victim in this case, and her name is Mita Cruz. This case should've never made it this far, but because of an over zealous District Attorneys office, my client has to relive the horrific experiences, which brings us here today. I will prove beyond reasonable doubt that my client deserves to live a normal life." He stared at the jury, making sure they saw the tears he allowed to escape from his eyes. He had the jury on the edge of their seats in complete suspense.

"Your Honor, the People call its first witness. Dr. Bill Sala, the Chief Medical Examiner for the City of Philadelphia."

A red, curly redheaded white man who was sixty pounds overweight took the stand, breathing heavily.

"Dr. Sala, would you please tell your Honor and the jury the causes of death in this case."

"Yes. Mrs. Sonia Cruz was stabbed over sixty-five times, repeatedly. Her cause of death was a stab wound to the jugular vein. It's also fair to say that she was beaten with a blunt object. Mr. Rafael Mendez was stabbed one time, directly in the heart. In my professional opinion, the murder weapon was a broken soda or beer bottle."

The District Attorney smiled as if he had already won the case.

Mr. Perry calmly got up from the defense table and stared at the judge before he walked over to the jury box. He wanted to make Dr. Sala sweat a little before he grilled him.

The jury was staring at Dr. Sala, no doubt wondering if this fat pig of a doctor was lying or not.

"Dr. Sala, you did perform an autopsy examination. Do you have that report in court today?"

"Yes, sir, I have it." Dr. Sala began to shake, looking at the District Attorney in distress. *Godamnit! You said you had this covered!*

"Please read it out loud for the court.

After Dr. Sala read his report to the courtroom, Mr. Perry asked, "One more question: What were the fact-findings?"

"Some of the fact findings were crack cocaine, heroin, and a number of prescribed medications. I also determined that both victims in this case were HIV positive."

"Why didn't you mention this in your testimony?"

The racist judge looked down at Dr. Sala from his holy bench and yelled, "Dr. Sala, answer the question!"

"Because I was informed by Mr. Vega that it was irrelevant to my testimony."

"Irrelevant! My client's life is on the line, and you think it's irrelevant?"

"Objection! Mr. Perry is harassing the witness!" the District Attorney chimed in.

"Sustained," the judge ordered.

Mr. Perry was on fire. He wanted to crush the District Attorney and get this shit over with quick. Bigger and better cases awaited him. He had struck a book and film deal with some Hollywood big wig who was trying to produce his life story for the LifeTime Network.

"Your Honor, the defense calls Mr. Gilberto "El Bodegero" Colon to the stand."

El Bodegero was Mr. Perry's ace in the hole. I was fuming as I watched this pervert stroll into the courtroom without a worry in the world. He had struck a sweet deal with the District

Attorney for immunity. In return, he had testified in a triple homicide, which took place in front of his establishment. His testimony resulted in two death sentences, so now the District Attorney was indebted to him. Even though Mr. Vega didn't want him to testify for the defense, there was little he could do to prevent it.

El Bodegero saw this opportunity as way of cashing in the one favor owed to him by the system. Little did he know that the devil he had made a deal with would flip-flop faster then Sara Palin. If I had another beer bottle at hands' reach, I would've shoved it up his ass right in the courtroom.

The bailiff swore El Bodegero in. "Sir, please raise your right hand and place your left hand on the Bible. Do you swear to tell the truth, the whole truth and nothing but the truth?" If looks could kill, El Bodegero would've been dead, because the bailiff gave him a look that was felt across the Criminal Justice Center.

"Mr. Colon, has anybody threatened you or made any promises to you in exchange for your testimony?"

"No!" El Bodegero was determined to get his fifteen minutes of fame.

"In your own words, would you please tell Your Honor and the jury what brings you here today? Please don't be afraid to be explicit. We want to know the truth and nothing but the truth." Mr. Perry was treating this perverted asshole with respect to make him feel comfortable.

"I'm known in the neighborhood as El Bodegero. I've

known the defendant since she was a little girl. I was a good friend of her family as well, I--" Before he was able to complete what he was about to spit out of his month, he broke down crying like a lil' bitch.

"Take your time, sir. I know it's difficult," Mr. Perry said as he stood in front of the witness stand and offered El Bodegero his Stacy Adams, four hundred dollar handkerchief and a glass of water, which was a class act.

"As I was saying, the defendant used to come to my store like all the kids in the neighborhood did because I let them take what they wanted. The defendant was a regular. One day I decided to play a game with her in my office. I sat her on my lap and molested her, and made her pee on my penis. I just lost control of myself. I'm sorry! I'm sorry! Then one day her mother approached me with an opportunity of a life time, at least for a sick person like me. Her mother offered me her daughter in exchange for money. I went to her house and sexually assaulted her twice. I'm sorry! I'm really sorry! I'm--"

*Yeah? You also may be the father of my child!* I couldn't stand to hear this sick bastard re-tell how he had fucked me in detail. I suddenly jumped up from the table and before the deputies could restrain me, I cracked El Bodegero in the face with the water pitcher that was sitting on top of the defense table. "I hate you! I hate you! I hate you!" I yelled as the deputies dragged my ass out of the courtroom.

The judge was pissed that I'd interrupted his nut. All along while El Bodegero had been setting himself up for a rape case, the judge had been masturbating with a pump concealed under his black robe. *Godamnit! This pretty little spic is lucky I can't get my hands on her. She probably needs more dick up in her so she can act right.* The judge could care less about justice. All he wanted was to bust a nut while looking under my skirt from the bench.

After the courtroom was empty, the judge detached his wrinkled lil' dick from inside the pump and quickly put it inside his briefcase.

Mr. Perry was all smiles. This was the case that was going to turn him into an international celebrity, so he played his part to the hilt. Before the judge allowed the jury to be brought back into the courtroom, he gave me a lecture on courtroom behavior.

"Young lady, this is a courtroom, not a boxing ring. I will not tolerate any more of your nonsense. You will conduct yourself as a young lady. If you even dare to breathe hard, I will have the deputies cuff and shackle you up. Do you understand me?"

*Just sit there and open your legs and let me finish my nut!* the judge was thinking to himself.

"Yes, I understand you," I whispered in a sickeningly phony voice.

"Your Honor, the defense calls Mita Cruz to the stand. I advised her of her rights. She understands that by taking the stand, the District Attorney may want to cross examine her."

"If the defendant wants to take the stand, I'll allow it," the judge said, staring at me. He was probably coming all over his black robe.

Once I took the stand, I was able to see where all the

people in the courtroom were seated, and I was disgusted. These assholes were here to show support for me, but I wasn't buying it. Where were they when I was getting my ass beaten and raped? I couldn't stand the sight of them ma'fuckas. By the expression on my attorney's face, I knew he wanted me to tell the truth. Believe me, the opportunity to do so was the only reason why I had agreed to take the stand. I tilted my head forward, and a few tears escaped my eyes. My voice was shaking, but I was determined to make myself clear, so I placed the microphone directly in front of me.

"Ladies and gentlemen of the jury, I give you Mita Cruz," Mr. Perry said.

I took a deep breath, and an image of Rafael appeared in my mind. A bitter sound erupted from my throat. "Ever since I could remember, my mother, Sonia Cruz, and stepfather, Rafael Mendez, were abusive towards me--spiting on me, kicking me, not feeding me, molesting me, and trading me off to all kinds of different men for money and drugs. I remember trying to commit suicide because I didn't want to be around them, and I was only nine years old. When I turned fourteen, my mother allowed my stepfather to rape me and take my virginity. She said it was my birthday present..." I paused, closed my eyes and swallowed the knot in my throat. "My childhood was nothing I'm proud of. Three weeks after my stepfather raped me, my mother allowed El Bodegero to rape me also for crack money. That was the day I ran away, but the damage was done. I was pregnant. Lucky for me, Mrs. Penny took me in and cared for me as if she was my mother."

A slight gasp from someone in the gallery echoed throughout the courtroom.

"By the time I was ready to give birth to my daughter, my mother reappeared, walked into the maternity ward, snatched my baby away from me and gave it up for adoption. It wasn't enough for her that she allowed her only child to be raped twice, but then she wanted to take my child. It was easy for me to kill both of them. I hated them. I did society a favor. I killed two evil animals. If I had known how easy it was, I would've done it a long time ago. If you want to send me to prison, you can. At least I know I'd be safe and not raped." When I was done telling my story, complete silence fell on the courtroom.

"Your Honor, may the People cross examine? It will be fast. The State only has a few questions," Mr. Vega said with a devious smile.

"Yes, you may," the judge replied.

"Ms. Cruz, I'm sorry to hear about your traumatic experiences, but I have a few questions for you, okay? Did you ever love your mother?"

"Yes, I did. At one time there was nothing I wouldn't have done just to get a hug from her. Yes, I did love my mother."

"If you loved your mother as you're proclaiming, then why did you kill her? Why didn't you go to the police instead?"

"Are you serious? What would the police have done?"

"They could've protected you from all the abuse you claim you were suffering," he said with a smile, as if I was making this shit up.

"Everyone in this courtroom knows what goes on in my neighborhood. I'm not the first or the last person who's been raped or sold out for crack. This is an everyday occurrence in my neighborhood. Children's Services knows what goes on, but ask them how many times they visited my house. Ask them why they didn't protect me. I did what I had to do to protect myself."

"Do you feel remorseful?"

"No, I don't. I'd do it again if I had to."

The judge looked at me as if I was crazy. My lawyer walked up to the witness stand and wrapped his hands around me, and led me back to the defense table. All the reporters and cameras were directed at me, and Mr. Perry had a big ass smile on his face, as if he had just won the case. Then, all hell broke loose.

"Quiet in the courtroom! Quiet in the courtroom!" The judge banged his gavel on the bench. "If I hear another outburst, I will have the deputies clear the courtroom out!" Then he added, "If the People or defense don't have any more witnesses, I will allow both parties to give their closing arguments."

"Your Honor, the defense is prepared for closing arguments." Mr. Perry wanted to get this trial over with. He was more interested in being famous than getting me off the hook. "Ladies and gentleman of the jury, I ask you to please study the evidence. You heard the witnesses, and nothing in this case shows that the defendant planned these acts. The defendant was severely raped, abused, sold out to different men for drugs by her own mother. What would you have done if you were in her shoes? If you believe in justice, then I ask you to acquit the defendant and get her treatment." Mr. Perry kept it short and simple.

"Ladies and gentlemen of the jury, I ask you to please not let the defendant's baby face fool you. Yes, her story of abuse is heartfelt, but we are not here for that. This is not an abuse case, this is a manslaughter case. These are nothing but allegations. There is nothing on record to support her claims. However, the evidence in this case shows that the defendant took it upon herself to bring justice according to her belief. The evidence shows that the defendant killed her mother and stepfather because she didn't want to obey the house rules her mother had put in place. We can't allow our youth to just take justice into their own hands. Mrs. Cruz and Mr. Mendez deserve justice. I'm asking you to do the right thing and find the defendant guilty as charged."

It took the jury less then three hours to determine ray fate. I glanced over at my lawyer. He appeared confident, as he had since the trial began.

The judge looked over at me with a perverted smile. "Will the defendant please rise." He then addressed the jury foreman. "Has the jury reached a verdict?"

"Yes, Your Honor. We find the defendant guilty."

I felt as if I've been raped over all over again. The spectators in the courtroom went bananas.

"Quiet! Quiet in the courtroom!" the judge shouted, ordering the deputies to cuff me up immediately. "Young lady, my hands are tied, and I'm mandated by law to sentence you to twenty-one years in the State prison. I hereby turn you over to the custody of the Department of Corrections."

This shit was like a bad dream. I looked at the jury and shook my head in amazement. Twelve members of my community decided my fate, and not one of them had the courage to look me in the eyes... not one. My hellish ordeal meant nothing to them. Ironically, El Bodegero ended up doing five months on probation for raping me. Being the real victim, I ended up with a one-way ticket to Muncie Correctional Facility, located in the boondocks of Pennsylvania.

# Part Two

# CHAPTER 7

## "Twenty-One Years Later/A New Beginning"

The urge to feel a long hard dick up in my stomach was overwhelming. I had only been penetrated by a man twice in my life, and those two times were under extreme circumstances. So yes, my pussy was very tight. You couldn't blame me for wanting some dick up in me. Twenty-one years was a long time to go without sex. I felt like a fucking nun. I won't front, in those years I ate me a lil' pussy. In fact, I became somewhat of an expert at it. Ain't no secret why they called me "Sweet Lips". By no means did I consider myself a dyke, but a bitch did what she had to do to survive. Some may have looked at my situation and considered me a dyke, but fuck it! As far as I was concerned, society could kiss my ass.

When I first arrived at Muncie State Correctional Institution, I was a young pretty bitch surrounded by a bunch of booty bandits. The dykes in here were going crazy fighting each other over who was gonna lick my tender luxury box first. In the beginning, I wasn't having it. I had to serve a few bitches some serious beat downs just to show them hoes that I wasn't soft or the one to be fucked with. I was bitter, angry and willing to kill again. I became the coldest bitch ever.

I didn't do twenty-one years of hard prison time dreaming. I prepared myself because I knew this day would arrive. It was over now. I didn't owe the State shit. They got all they were entitled to get out of me. In two hours, I'll be walking out of that jungle a free woman and a cold-hearted bitch on a mission. As the guard escorted me to the Assessment Unit to be fingerprinted and photographed, I couldn't contain myself. I creamed in my panties. For me, this would be my first breath of fresh air since the age of fourteen.

The fat nasty looking white chick who was escorting me to Assessment seemed jittery. I had acquired a reputation in Muncie for being a tough ass bitch, with the best pussy eating game in the system. I'd been convicted of only one crime, manslaughter, which I proudly confessed to without blinking an eye. Finally, when we reached the assessment unit, reality sank in. I smiled, feeling the wetness between my thighs. This was the day I had been waiting for.

"Ms. Cruz, fingerprinting and photographing are a routine process for all inmates being released. Face the X marked on the wall to the right. Turn to the left and look straight at the camera." The sloppy, *chi-chi* eating guard had a high pitched tone to her voice.

I posed for the photos as if I was a model posing for the "Eye Candy" section of the *King* Magazine. I gave the camera a seductive stare, while all alone blowing kisses.

"Ms. Cruz, we can do this the easy way, or we can do it the hard way. However you want to do it. We have until midnight to hold you," she mumbled.

I just stared at her, giving her the *"Bitch, please!"* look. This nasty freak can't tell me what to do no more. I'm maxing out. However, these tricks may try to hold me 'til midnight, so let me chill.

The guard was taking her sweet ass time, acting like the camera was out of film. She was really fantasizing about a sexual escapade. It was known inside of Muncie that female guards exchanged favors for sex, and since I had the best brain game, I'd benefited the most. Believe me, guards and inmates alike were kicking out heavy paper for some Sweet Lips.

*Only if this fly bitch would hit me off one last time,* the guard thought to herself as she felt her pussy growing moist.

*Bitch! Your nasty ass will never get a taste of these Sweet Lips ever again!*

"Okay, Ms. Cruz, you can go into the next room for fingerprinting."

I just smiled and bounced my fat as into the next room. Fingerprinting only took a few minutes.

"Ms. Cruz, I have a few questions, and then you will be on your way. Do you have any money in your inmate account?"

With a big ass smile, I replied, "Yes, more than I can count." I was proud of the fact that I was able to save up twenty five stacks while locked up, enough to have a head start at life. I wasn't trying to hit the bricks dead-ass broke like so many inmates do, which forced them to turn back to the street game. Plus, Mrs. Penny left me a lil' something in her Will before she succumbed to ovarian cancer.

The guard paused, then handed me a pair of blue jeans and a blue jacket.

"Nah, I got my own clothes. Would you please check in the storage room? My counselor informed me yesterday that my clothes were here." I handed her a pink confiscation slip. Within minutes, she returned with a box containing my clothes. *Bitch gotta be ass crazy to think I'm walking out of this place with the same clothes I wore for twenty-one years! I wouldn't be caught dead in that shit!*

I ripped the box open, slipped out of my prison browns and kicked them to the side. Then I took off my jailhouse panties and stood naked in front of the guard. It didn't matter that a male guard was in the room. After a while in prison, you get used to stripping naked, 'cause guards constantly want to strip a bitch nude. It's a form of humiliation. I wasn't trying to take nothing with me that reminded me of prison.

Once I slipped into my new faded black Hudson jeans, my black Dior flip-flops and a white and pink Dior Tee, compliments of all the Internet pen-pals who'd been blessing me with fat ass money orders throughout the years, I was ready to face the world. The guard handed me a check with an evil smile. The only worldly possessions I owned were the clothes on my back. I walked out of Muncie looking like Vida Guerra.

"Hey, Cruz, don't forget to send a Christmas card! Or better yet, come back and visit!" one guard said sarcastically and laughed.

"Don't hate, congratulate! But don't worry, I'll make sure I send you a card full of cum when I get my first nut, bitch!"

The reality was that ninety percent of the inmates who got released from prison returned to prison within six months to a year. The odds were against me. I had no family or support system waiting to embrace me, but I was determined.

I stared at the Iron Gate, waiting for it to swing open and give me a taste of Pennsylvania's fresh air, something I'd been waiting twenty-one years for. When the gate opened, I walked out of Muncie, bouncing my ass to the rhythm of my own beat.

At thirty-five, I'd been given a new lease on life. I had lost my innocence twice in my life: When I was raped, and when I was sent to prison. My entire youth was left behind in Muncie State Prison, but I did discover a new woman while there; the coldest bitch ever.

Unfortunately, my daughter, was twenty-one years old now, probably wouldn't say the same. According to all the information I had managed to gather, she was put up for adoption right after birth, something I already knew. I was still fucked up how Sonia just took my child away from me. Even though all these years had passed, I still felt the pain of not being able to hold my own daughter. Now, I was committed to locating my bloodline. *Damn! I don't even know what my daughter looks like!* Those morbid thoughts flashed back into my mind, and no matter how hard I tried to suppress them, they were unavoidable.

One look at me, and no one would ever image I had been incarcerated for twenty-one years.

When the two red-neck guards who were escorting me to the bus stop arrived, I got out of the car and gave both of them crackers the middle finger as I walked up the steps into the bus station to begin my ride back to North Philadelphia, a free woman. Nobody on the bus gave me the dirty stares they normally give the inmates who were dropped off at this particular bus stop, waiting to be shipped back to a life of destruction and recidivism.

When the bus reached King of Prussia Shopping Mall, I smiled. It was 9:30 p.m. I was fully awake, anticipating my return to my birthplace. No one was going to stop me from executing my plans. I was on some C.B.S. (Can't Be Stopped) shit. I had goals to achieve, dicks to suck, pussies to lick, money to grab and a daughter to locate. *Thirty five more miles, and I'm home!*

Half an hour later when the bus pulled up at 12th and Filbert, my panties were wet. I exited the bus, leaving any link to Muncie State prison behind.

Downtown Philadelphia was jam packed with all types of low life ma'fuckas plotting on tourists, and lames who wanted to floss their hard-earned money, with hopes of catching themselves a hoodrat for the night.

With the exception of a few new buildings, the structure of the city of Brotherly Love was still the same. Since I didn't have any cash on hand, I entertained myself by window shopping, making mental notes of all the stores I wanted to visit once I was able to cash my check in the morning. It was 1:30 in the morning, and I was just happy to be able to walk the streets without having a bitch ass guard telling me what to do. A few fine niggas tried to holla at me, but I kept it moving. I walked the streets of Philly with a purpose. When the sun started to rise, I made my way to the City National Bank on Market Street.

"Good morning. May I help you with something?" the teller asked as he eyed me up and down, staring long and hard at my cleavage.

"Yes. I would like to open an account and deposit a check," I said in a flirtatious manner.

The teller nodded. "First, you have to fill out this application, and if you want an ATM card, please indicate it on your application."

"May I use your pen, sir?" I bent over the counter, giving him a view of my *tetas* (titties). Once I was done using the pen, I handed it back to him, purposely rubbing his hand. Despite the fact that he looked like a young square, I knew that befriending him could be beneficial to me in the long run. Plus, what square nigga wouldn't want to be seen with a hot chick? The power of pussy can have a nigga do back flips in a heartbeat.

"Here you go, Miss," the teller said, handing me three thousand dollars in cash and my new bankbook, along with his business card.

I looked at the business card and smiled. "I thank you kindly, Mr. Solomon," I said seductively. As I was about to exit the bank, I turned around and interrupted his fantasy dream. "One more question. Can I call you from time to time? Maybe you can guide me in the right direction concerning my finances.

I would appreciate any help you could give me."

"Sure! You can call me whenever you'd like. It's an honor for me to be able to help and welcome such a beautiful lady like you to the city. Don't hesitate to use my number."

"Thank you, sweetie," I replied. I then dropped my bankbook on the floor on purpose, and bent over to give him a good thirty-second view of my perfectly round ass. I knew right there and then that I was gonna break this nigga down with some pussy. He was gonna be my backup cash flow. Shit! And maybe I could have his dumb ass set me up in an apartment! Maybe I was jumping the gun, but one thing was for sure, I was gonna give him a taste of my Sweet Lips.

Working wasn't part of my plans. Although I had earned a B.S. Degree from Penra State University in Business Communications while I was in the joint, I wasn't about to give anyone authority over me. Fuck that! Plus, who was gonna hire an ex-con?

After I exited the bank, I went straight to an apartment duplex and rented a studio apartment. Half an hour later, I had my own place to lay my head. It wasn't anything fancy, but it was paid up for the next six months, and I didn't have to share it with no nasty bitch. The nine by twelve-foot cell that I called home for the last twenty-one years couldn't compete with my new place of residence.

Once I had the keys to my apartment, I went back out the door. Center City was jam packed with the early morning traffic. A mixture of all races were combined together. The rich and the poor, the working class, street bums, hookers, gold diggers, and the low classes, they all looked like they were in a hurry. *I'm not gonna be one of them.*

I found my way to the Gallery Mall, and bought myself a brand new wardrobe. It didn't matter to me if the clothes were top of the line designers or not. Once I put them on, they would look like they were worth something. My exotic Latina looks alone made me look like a star. My long, jet-black hair and my light brown cat eyes always turned people on, men and women alike. My distinctive heart shaped lips put me in a class of my own. My skin was flawless. Standing at five feet five, my body was tight from all the running and sit ups I'd done in prison. My D-cup breasts were firm, and my fat ass was super tight. My hips could have been insured for a million dollars, curving from my small waist. Nobody needed to tell me that I was definitely a dime piece.

With shopping out of the way, I returned to my apartment, threw all the bags on top of the bed, stripped down naked and hopped into the bathtub, something I'd been waiting to do for a long time. *Damn! I feel like a natural woman!* I thought as I laid my head back to let the warm water soak into my body. I was feeling sensual. I stayed in the bathtub for a half hour.

When I finally got out, I was ready to catch up with the world. I sat down on the edge of the bed asshole naked, making a list of things to do, places to visit, and people to see. On top of that list was the Department of Human Services.

Twenty four hours into my release from prison, I was

already on my way to rebuilding my life. A new wardrobe, a nice clean studio apartment, a fat bank account, and a potential sugga *papi*. What else could an ex-con ask for, when just yesterday, I was locked up, wishing on a star?

Philly was the city that watched me grow up for fourteen years. This is the city that treated me as a criminal and victimized me twice... the city that stole my innocence. Now it was the city that was going to watch me become the most vindictive bitch. Why not? A lil' revenge could only even the score. The mindset I'd developed in prison was fuck the world! It's all about me. Trust no one, and there was no way I could fail.

With hardly any sleep since gaining my freedom, I wasn't even tired or hungry. To me, sleeping wasn't an option. I'd slept twenty-one years of my life, and I wasn't about to waste anymore time sleeping. A minute spent sleeping was a minute spent doing nothing.

After planning my next move, I slowly got off of the bed, slid my hourglass figure into a pair of Alan B. Jeans, some Christian Louboutine with the cork platforms, a fresh white T, and I completed my outfit with an oversized YSL black leather bag. Feeling good about myself, I grabbed some money, my keys, and I.D. and headed out the door. First, I was gonna get me something to grub on, and then I was gonna visit my old neighborhood.

I sat in the back of a small cafe, enjoying the loud chatter of the patrons, and the skinny white waitress who looked like she couldn't handle the loud noise. I stayed focused on the plate of food the waitress put on the table in front of me. This was the first meal I was enjoying as a free woman, and I felt empowered, knowing I could choose whatever I wanted to eat without anyone telling me no. The last time I was free, I was too young to even buy a pack of cigarettes, and all my moves were controlled by my mother. In prison, the food was pure trash. I groaned with excitement when I let my tongue taste the deep fried chicken and French fries. "This gotta be the best chicken I've ever eaten!"

"The best in the city!" the waitress said with a wide grin.

All I could do was nod my head as I took another bite. When I was done, in my haste to get on with my plans, I took a deep breath, plied off a one hundred-dollar bill, handed it to the waitress and simply walked out of the cafe.

"Miss! Miss! You forgot your change!" the waitress yelled once she caught up with me outside.

"No, I didn't forget. Consider it your tip," I replied with a proud smile.

The waitress just stared at me. Most of her tips were in the range of two or three dollars. Never before had anyone given her an eighty-six dollar tip.

*I'm willing to bet this ugly bitch never got a tip this large. The heifer ran after me thinking I forgot my change.*

I headed towards Broad Street, enjoying the summer breeze. Within a half hour I was standing in front of the house that transformed my life forever; 2731 North Erie Avenue still looked the same, Nothing had really changed. I considered knocking on the door and asking permission to look inside the only house I had ever known, but discarded that notion. "Not today, *Mami*, you dirty ass whore!" My curiosity had been satisfied. I have no remorse for killing my mother and stepdad, and nor would I ever be sorry. In fact, I'd do it again if I had to. *They got what they deserved!*

Walking down Erie Avenue brought back childhood memories, especially when I stopped in front of El Bodegero's store. I wanted to keep walking, but I couldn't. I needed to see if El Bodegero was still up to his old tricks. When I walked in, the store was filled with little schoolgirls and boys, and El Bodegero was behind the counter slobbering all over his fat self. How the fuck does society allow a monster like him to run freely around children? I wanted to spit in his face, but in due time he would get his. The son of a bitch didn't even recognize me when I went up to the counter and paid for a soda. He was too busy trying to look up some little girl's skirt.

When I returned to my apartment, I was feeling a little overwhelmed. Never again would I allow anyone to abuse me. For no particular reason, tears started pouring down my face. I just lay on my belly and drifted off to sleep. When I awoke, it was morning.

# CHAPTER 8

### "Doing It My Way"

I strolled into the Department of Human Services, located in Center City as if I was Sasha Fierce, aka Beyonce, hoping to find directions on where I could start looking for my daughter. I wasn't in the office a minute when I was approached by a fine ass Puerto Rican chick who almost made me forget the purpose of my being there.

"*Hola! Como esta?* Can I help you with anything?" the chick, whose name was Inez asked while licking her lips.

"Yes, you can. My name is Mita Cruz, and twenty-one years ago I gave birth to a baby girl whose name I don't know. She was snatched from me and put up for adoption by my parents. I'm wondering if you can help me find her or put me on the right track," I replied with a bright smile.

"Ms. Cruz, first of all, the Department of Human Services is prohibited by law from revealing any information concerning adoptions. Most of the time, if the child is not adopted within the first ninety days of birth; they linger in the foster care system until they turn eighteen years old. If your daughter is twenty-one now, she's most likely out on her own. Maybe you should try the Internet," the girl said in a professional manner. But I wasn't trying to hear her suggestions.

"So there is nothing you can do for me, right?"

"No, not really. As I said, we are not allowed to reveal any information concerning adoptions."

"But just because you're not allowed doesn't mean you can't," I blared out, growing frustrated.

Inez understood where this chick was coming from, because she was a product of the foster care system. For the first eight years of her life she suffered countless sexual assaults, vicious ass whippings, and neglect. At the age of ten she was legally adopted by a middle-class Hispanic Family. For the first three months, life seemed promising, until one night her adopted father walked into her room butt ass naked and fucked her lil' brains out.

"Don't worry, baby. *Papi* is going to be good to you. Haven't I been good to you so far? Haven't you enjoyed yourself in this house? Be good to me and I'll be good to you. If you act up, I promise I'll send you back to foster care, so come here and give *Papi* a lil' suga."

Mr. Rodriguez knew how to deal with these little foster girls who were in need of a happy home. At forty-two years old, he and his wife, Rosa made a living taking in foster kids and adopting them. The State paid them a healthy check twice a month for each child they took in. Rosa knew her husband was fucking the shit out of all the little girls in the house, but since none of them ever complained to the social worker, she looked the other way. Those who did complain were viewed as trouble makers, and were never believed.

Rosa Rodriguez was a nasty, flabby looking Puerto Rican woman who looked like a drag queen from hell. She had hair growing under her chain. At 5"6', 280 pounds of jelly, the sight of her was enough to scare any man away. No wonder Mr. Rodriguez was fucking all the little girls in their care.

Rosa had been given a distinguished award by Philadelphia City Mayor Michael Nutter for being the foster mother who had demonstrated the most care and unconditional love for the children she cared for, and Mr. Rodriguez had been awarded Foster Father of the Year. Yet behind closed doors, they were both two disgusting, unfit drunks.

At ten years old, Inez was developing quickly. She was wearing a C-cup bra, and her little booty was getting fatter and fatter by the hour. In school, she would tell the older boys that she was fourteen years old, and no one ever questioned me.

"Get naked, *hija,* (daughter) so *Papi* can get a good look at you."

She obliged. Through her journey in foster care, she had been sexually assaulted four times, so she knew this was to be expected if she wanted to stay in a halfway stable home. Once she was naked, she dropped to her knees and did what she'd been doing since she could remember, giving her adopted father the best blow job the no good bastard ever had. She gave him facial expressions and all.

He was dizzy. *Rosa don't even get me this excited. Hell! She can't suck half as good as this little hoe.* "Make sure you swallow, *nena* (girl)!"

Inez looked at him with her dark brown eyes and smiled. Once he busted his nut, he rolled her over on my stomach and sodomized her. Inez took the pain like a champion. She would rather have had a little pain in her *culo* (ass) than be sent back to foster care. Once her adopted father finished getting dressed, he bent down and kissed her on the forehead.

"*Papi*, before you leave, can you give me some money so I can buy some new sneakers?" Inez asked as she reached for the zipper of his pants and pulling it up for him.

"Sure. How much money you need?"

"Like a hundred dollars."

"A hundred dollars!"

"Yes. I'm good for it, right?" she said and licked her lips.

He pulled out his wallet and gave me a crispy one hundred-dollar bill. "*Nena*, don't tell your mother I gave you money. She would flip out on me, so keep your mouth shut, okay, sweetie?"

Three abortions and seven years later, Inez's adopted father was still dipping into her hidden treasure; only now he was no longer in control. She was calling the shots, and was taking his perverted ass to the bank on some blackmail shit. She threatened to expose him if he didn't break her off with half of the monthly check they were receiving. Inez had recorded them abusing all the girls in the house, and she had enough footage to put "Ray J and Kim Kardashian" out of business.

Her plans were to one day bring down the foster care system in Philadelphia. But since she was as scandalous as they come and a hardcore dyke on a pussy hunt, she took the opportunity to try and get some pussy from the fine chick in front of her. "Listen, I'm just doing my job, so don't get mad at me. Plus, you are the one who needs the help, not me. So don't give me no attitude. Now that we have an understanding, I may be able to help you, but not here."

This young chick's aggressiveness had shocked me somewhat. Nevertheless, I recognized her weak ass game a mile away, and I decided to play along because I needed the help. This young bitch was trying to crack on the pussy in a professional manner. "If not here, where?"

"Here is my number. Call me today at four o'clock. We can get together and do dinner, on me." Inez said, going for the jugular.

"I'd watch my wishes if I were you, but it sounds like a perfect plan to me," I responded. It would have been damned difficult not to notice that Inez was trying to bag me. I was willing to play whatever game she wanted to play, just as long as I got what the fuck I wanted.

I spent that afternoon visiting various landmark institutions in the city; The Liberty Bell, Love Park, and Geno's Cheese Steaks, which is where I met this lame ass nigga named Suso. I won't front, the nigga had the appearance of a balla, and he was fine. He resembled the rapper, Nas, but as we all know, looks can be deceiving.

When I reached the front of the line, I contemplated not ordering, once I read the sign Geno's had posted on the front window that read, "When placing an order, you must speak English! This is America!" *These racist bastards!* My thoughts were interrupted when the young Nas look-alike mustered up enough *cajones* (balls) to approach me.

"Excuse me, Miss, I'm willing to pay for your order if you allow me a minute of your time."

*This gotta be the most weak ass line I ever heard. I'll pay for your order! Four dollars and fifty cents! This nigga better keep it moving!* "Nah, I'm safe. I don't need you to pay for my order. My time is worth more than four dollars and fifty cents," I said, not even bothering to look at this clown.

"Damn, Ma! I meant no disrespect. I was just trying to be a gentleman, but don't get it twisted. I'm willing to pay whatever amount your time is worth." Suso pulled out a fat ass bankroll and added, "It ain't tricking if you got it."

"Are you serious?"

"Yeah, I'm serious."

"Am I supposed to be impressed?" I asked him, curling my lips up in a heart shape, sizing Suso up. Once I noticed his dick print, I knew he was full of lust. His weakness was pussy. *I'ma test this young nigga gangster since he wants to front like he's Jim Jones, ballin'. "It ain't tricking if you got it!" Nigga's gonna have to come off that bankroll if he wants some conversation.*

"Naw, I'm not trying to impress you, I just wanna know your name. So, what's up?"

"As I stated, my time is worth money."

"How much?"

"How much time are we talking about?"

"A few minutes."

"Two hundred dollars per minute."

"Damn, Ma! Dat's a lot of money for some conversation. All I want to know is your name."

I knew I had this lame ass nigga mesmerized, because he was still standing in front of me and fronting like a ma'fucka.

"A'ight, here you go." Suso peeled off ten one hundred big faces from his bankroll and handed them to me. "Dat should cover a good five minutes," he stated, confident of his ability to have me all over him like most chicken heads in the 'hood.

"Five minutes, huh?" I whispered as I handed the man behind the Plexiglas one of the bills Suso gave me.

*I know dis bitch didn't just gave this cracker my money, when I just offered to pay for her order! Bitch got balls for real!*

"You're on the clock, young boy. Time is money," I said as I folded the rest of the money he gave me and slid the wad inside my bag.

"What's your name?"

"Sweet Lips," I responded seductively, curling my lips into a heart shape.

"Where are you from? I never seen you around here."

"I'm new in town, but I'm originally from Puerto Rico," I lied. This nigga didn't need to know much about me.

"I'm a Philly Rican, but my people are from Puerto Rico."

"In other words, you're *chapio!*"

"Nah, Ma, a hundred percent *Boriqua* (Puerto Rican)."

*Nigga, please!* "So, you a balla... a drug dealer, right?"

"Naw, I work hard for my chips. How about you?"

"I'm a therapist."

"Really! Damn, you on some Dr. Phil shit? Dat shit is hot!"

"Dr. Phil is a clown. I'm a sex therapist," I said with a hint of mischievous smile, watching him lust off my ass.

"Damn, Ma! Has anyone ever told you dat you look like the Cuban chick, Vida Guerra?"

"Naw. But if she looks this hot, then I accept your complement."

"How old are you, Ma?"

"A woman never tells her age, but I'm old enough to do grown folks' things." *Two more minutes of this corny nigga spitting weak-ass game...*

"Since your new in town, you gonna need a personal tour guide to show you around, and I'm available and willing. How about if we hook up later on so I can show you around town?"

"I said I'm new in the city, not lonely. I'm not really interested in meeting new people. I'm sure a fly *young boy* like you has plenty of women throwing their panties at you." I made sure to emphasize the words "young boy" just to see his reaction.

"I'm not a young boy, Ma. I'm twenty two years old-old and old enough to do grown folks' things," he said with a smile.

"My bad! I meant no disrespect to you." A badly bruised ego can hurt just as much as a broken heart. When one is young, stupid and vulnerable, mistakes are made, and this young lame ass nigga had made the mistake of biting off more than he could chew.

"Since my time is almost up, can I at least get your phone number? I may need more therapy," he asked.

"I don't have a phone, but if you give me your number, I promise I'll call you as soon as I get one." I watched his nostrils flare. The expression on his face was like that of a man in need of a good shot of that gushy stuff. His light brown eyes were glaring down at my fat ass.

"I'ma be waiting on your call. Here's my number."

"Thank you, sweetie."

"Your welcome, Ma."

"By the way, young boy, you should be more careful out here!" I called him young boy again on purpose, not giving him a chance to respond while I walked away with a wet pussy and a stack richer. Here I was, telling this lame to be careful, but it was too late. He just ran into a mother's worst nightmare--the most scandalous, unstable bitch to ever touch the streets of Philly. I had every intention of taking this young nigga out of all his cash. You see, if a bitch plays her cards right, she can have any nigga out on the hoe-strip hustling for her, and niggas with egos will go the extra mile just to be able to get into some exclusive panties. And no bullshit, I'm as exclusive as they come. I was inclined to look back at him just to see his nut ass drooling all over himself. His weak ass game had collapsed under my pressure.

*Damn! I wouldn't mind paying for a shot of dat pussy! I'd suck her asshole! I got to have dat!* Suso thought to himself as he watched her walk away.

As soon as I made it back to Center City, I went into Circuit City and bought me a Motorola cell phone. Then I programmed this young lame's number into it.

# CHAPTER 9
## "Can I Talk To You?"

*"Riiiiiiing!"*

Inez let her phone ring more times than she should have. She didn't want me to think she was desperate, but I knew she was. I had read the bitch like a book earlier, but I was willing to play the game.

"Hello?" Inez said nonchalantly, looking at her watch. *Four o'clock on the dot! I'm good!* she thought as she answered the phone.

"Can I speak to Inez?"

"May I ask whose calling?"

The bitch tried to sound formal. "Mita Cruz."

"Oh, hi! I didn't recognize your voice."

*How could you, when your young ass is trying to put your dyke game down?* "Thank you for assisting me in this matter. I appreciate any help I can get," I probed.

"Well, I haven't been of any assistance yet," Inez said.

"I know, but so far you've been the only person willing to help me. It's a start."

"I hear you! Why don't I come pick you up so we can discus this issue over dinner to see where we can start? Where do you live?"

*Wait a minute! Who the fuck is this chick? As far as I'm concerned, this could be a setup! She could be a trifling ass thief of a whore. I don't know about this. The bitch might be crazy.* "You can pick me up at the Painted Bride Art Center down on South Street in about fifteen minutes. Is that cool with you?"

"Yeah, I know where it's at. I mean, is that your place of residency?"

"No, but if you want this dinner date to jump off, it's where you're going to meet me. By the way, I'm only willing to wait a few minutes, so don't have me waiting there looking all stupid," I said with a slight attitude, testing her pimp game.

"I hear you, Ma. Don't get all uptight and shit. It ain't that serious."

"Fifteen minutes started three minutes ago, and you're still on the phone. I'll see you in a few." I flipped the phone off, ran upstairs to my studio apartment to change my panties and shirt and freshen up a lil', then headed out the door. I only lived three minutes walking distance from the Painted Bride Art Center. I wanted to stay in public in case this bitch turned out to be crazy.

I stood in front of the Bride Art Center five minutes early, when I spotted a S550 Mercedes Benz heading in my direction. I thought to myself, *She has it going on! I know working at the Department of Human Services ain't paying for all that.*

Once the Benz stopped in front of me, Inez rolled the window down and said, "Hop in before one of those Parking Authority, hating ass bitches creeps up and writes me a ticket."

The thought of riding shotgun with a stranger I just met a

few hours ago left me with an itchy desire.

"You ever heard of Isla Verde Restaurant?" Inez asked me, interrupting my thoughts.

"Nah."

"Well, come on. I'm hungry. They got the best Spanish food in the city." Inez's mouth was starting to get watery, but not at the thought of Spanish food; she wanted to sink her teeth into my coochie. She had lust written all over her angelic face.

When we entered Isla Verde down on American and Lehigh Avenue, we were greeted by the owner, a stocky built Puerto Rican *papi* named Ray Pastrana, who was known around the city for his business skills and charming ways with the ladies.

Inez had first met Ray when she became the head hostess at Isla Verde. Soon after, she was fucking Ray's brains out. Ray introduced her to the lavish life, connecting her to some of the most powerful people in the city. He had kept her under his wing because she had demonstrated to him that she was a ride or die kind of chick.

Once seated in a booth in the VIP section, Ray leaned forward and said, "*Mi casa es su casa* (My house is your house). Anything you y'all desire is complimentary of Isla Verde. The waitress will take your orders when you're ready."

Inez winked at him for his generosity.

"This almost feels like I'm on a date," I whispered, testing the waters. I wanted to see Inez's reaction.

"It is a date. We both have ulterior motives. That's why we're here. I mean, we don't really know each other that well yet, but I'm looking forward to knowing you well enough by the end of the night."

Inez wasn't beating around the bush. She figured that if I wasn't getting up and leaving, then I must have been game. "So, how exactly can you help me in my search for my daughter?" I asked her.

"I'm not sure yet. We can put our heads together and think of a plan," Inez replied with a lustful smirk.

"Sounds like a good start to me. Tell me, Inez, does working at the Department of Human Services pay all your bills? I mean it looks like you got it going on."

"That's just my day job. I also have a night hustle. I fuck rich and powerful old men for money. Some people call it prostitution; others call it an escort service. Me, I call it living the lavish life--the best of both worlds. DHS is only good for the benefits. Fucking is what I do best. What do you do for a living?"

"Is that a question? I'm not the working kind of person, at least not at this moment." I didn't want to reveal too much of myself to this young chick. "Let's just say I inherited a nice chunk of money from a family member who passed away. That's how I survive."

"I see. You are one of those spoiled brats."

"Nah, I'm not a spoiled brat. I believe every woman deserves to be pampered."

"So, is there a special someone pampering you?" Inez asked with a smile.

"Not really. I'm a free agent. But back to the question at hand. How can you help me?"

"To be honest, I don't know, but I can definitely use my connections to find out certain things that these agencies out here won't tell you. Out of curiosity, why are you so persistent in locating your daughter after all these years?"

"Because I didn't have a say so in putting her up for adoption. I've never held her or even seen her."

"For real?"

"Yeah, for real. She was taken from me at birth. I don't even know her name. The only thing I know is her birthday. I remember it because it was one of the worst days of my life."

"Does your family support you in this search?"

"I don't have a family. My mother and father are both deceased and I'm an only child."

"I feel your pain, because I'm an only child also. I mean, I have adopted brothers and sisters, but they're not real family. Tomorrow I'll make a few phones calls and see what we can dig up. Do you know which hospital you gave birth in?"

"Yeah, Temple."

Just then, the waitress brought over some drinks and two delicious plates of Spanish food. Having dinner with Inez was making me feel like we could be friends. Inez was pure eye candy. She had light brown cat eyes like mine, long jet-black hair and a fat ass. I was willing to bet she had a shaved coochie. If she landed in prison, she wouldn't have any problems, 'cause one of those lesbo dykes would definitely be trying to wife her.

After speaking to her for a while, I realized I wouldn't mind having her for a sidekick. I tried to take it easy on the drinks because I had never drunk before. I was a virgin when it came to drinking.

"Want another drink?" Inez was practically salivating.

"Yup! Get me a gin with grapefruit juice." By the time I finished my second shot of gin, I was feeling super horny. Inez listened carefully to every word that came out of my mouth without interruption. For a half an hour we exchanged our views on men and our outlooks on life in general.

"I'm telling you, girl, I haven't been with a man in years! I don't even remember what a dick looks like, and I don't miss it either," I explained to Inez.

"You telling me you haven't had no dick in years? How do you get off?"

I was blunt with her. "For the most part, I kept a girlfriend on the side or I took care of myself. A sister must know how to fend for herself. You'd be surprised what magic these fingers can do," I said, waving my finger in a circular motion.

"I feel you, Ma!" Inez gave me a stern look, touching my hand. Her touch had me cumming in my panties. "Let me run somethin' down to you, Ma," she continued.

"What do you have in mind?"

"I want to spend the night with you. If you don't like what I'm offering, you can get up and bounce right now, and I'll still will help you locate your daughter. But right now, I just want to taste your pussy." She reached over and started licking and nibbling on my ear lobe. At the same time, she slid three fingers between my legs and into my already damp pussy.

"Umm! Ahhhhhhh!" I whispered out of pleasure, and then added, "How do you know I'm not a serial killer or something? Daaamn! That feels good!"

Inez had my clit on fire. It felt like it wanted to jump out of my pussy. The heat in the room was intense. Even as I tried to rub ice cubes across my face, my skin felt like it was on fire. It was her fingers on my clit that had me feeling like I was being tortured.

"The same can be said about me, but I'm willing to take a chance and risk it. How about you?"

"Life is about taking risks," I replied. Once I came, Inez pulled her wet fingers out of my pussy and licked them one at a time. Then she stuck her long hot tongue in my mouth, letting me taste my own pussy juices. Even if either one of us wanted to stop, we couldn't. The combination of liquor and the taste of pussy had both of our tongues on fire.

"I take chances every day, and you only live once. I have no regrets on how I'm living my life. Right now, you got my full attention," Inez whispered to me.

Inez was the kind of broad who needed to feel like she was in control, but if I had learned one thing in prison from dealing with those hardcore dykes, it was never to reveal your hand. Little did she know that eating pussy was my forte. For the time being, I let her believe her own pipe dreams.

"That being the case, I guess we can bounce," I told her.

"I guess so."

By the time I got up from my seat, pussy juice was dripping down my legs, and a big ass wet spot was embedded on the seat. "From now on, Inez, you can call me Sweet Lips. Mita is my government name," I blared out, forming my lips into a heart shape. I could swear I saw Inez's nipples harden, screaming for a taste of my sweet lips.

Inez was a young chick looking for a trophy to show off, and thought I was a stupid bitch looking for a one-night stand. I had peeped her game from the minute I walked into the Department of Human Services. This may sound melodramatic, but it's the literal truth: the bitch was about her pussy game on some real shit. But behind her brave and perilous adventures, she was a soft bitch who wished to be shielded from the harsh realities of life.

# CHAPTER 10
## "Da Power of the Pussy"

As we walked towards Inez's car, I couldn't help but feel curious about her. This young chick was hot as hell, pushing a Mercedes Benz, and sitting on some serious paper. She had to be doing more then just fucking for cash.

"Inez, do you normally sweet talk people into sleeping with you?" I stared straight into her eyes.

"Nah, just you." The smirk on her face wrote, "I Love Pussy!"

"Why me?"

"You're fine as hell! Your lips are the best I ever seen in a while."

"I've been told that before. You ain't that bad either."

"If you say so, but tonight it's all about you. How long you been in the city?"

"I was born here, and then I moved away for twenty-one years. Now I'm back to stay."

"Permanent or temporary?"

"Permanent," I responded, and ran my tongue across my lips.

"That's wassup!"

Inez leaned forward and locked her hot lips with mine.

She tried to keep up with my tongue action, but I was too much for the youngster. I sucked on her tongue as if it was a dick, and at the same time I returned the favor, sliding one finger into her pussy. "Bushy, huh?" I whispered as I ran my fingers softly across her pussy lips, making her whole body shiver. I stopped abruptly when I noticed a group of young niggas who seemed to be enjoying the sight of two hot chicks finger fucking and tongue fucking each other in public. "Let's wait until we get to the hotel. I'm not into giving free public shows." I pointed to the group of young guys, particularly the young boy who had his dick hanging out of his pants, yelling in our direction, "I got enough *bicho* (dick) for both of you bitches!"

Inez called the young boy who had his dick out over to her car, and he walked towards the passenger side and stuck his head inside the window. "So, you think you got enough dick to satisfy both of us?" she asked him. Then she slid a finger into my pussy and placed it in the young boy's mouth. "Pussy tastes good, don't it?"

"Yeah!" The young boy replied.

"But guess what, baby?"

"What?"

"Only in your dreams would you ever get to stick your nasty looking lil' dick in this pussy!" Inez pressed the gas pedal, sped off and left the young boy standing on the corner with his dick hanging out and leaking. I laughed so hard that tears rolled down my face.

The Philadelphia Marriott wasn't too far from Isla Verde,

so there wasn't too much time to waste. While Inez was driving, I sucked on my own nipples. From time to time when Inez would stop at the red light, she would stick one of my nipples into her mouth, biting it slightly. Then I would pull away slowly, letting the pool of saliva from her lips drip down my stomach.

When we pulled in front of the Philadelphia Marriott, we were both damn near naked. It took us a minute to straighten up.

When the doorman approached the car, the sweet smell of pussy gave him an instant hard-on. "Ladies, can I park your car for you?" The valet recognized me from Geno's Steak.

My mind was so far gone from thinking about Inez's pussy that I didn't even acknowledge him. As far as I was concerned, he was way below my level of desire.

No spoken words were necessary between Inez and me. We slowly walked into the Marriott holding hands like a couple. We smiled with pride after we noticed a few of the employees in the lobby staring at us. There was no denying it, Inez and I were two of the most beautiful Latina chicks to ever walk the streets of Philly, and we were bound by the same dirty little secret.

Inez immediately called for room service. She ordered vodka, lemon juice, ice cubes and strawberry ice cream. Once we were inside the suite, I watched her from the corner of my eye as she bent over to play with the stereo system. When the melodic soulful sounds of Marvin Gaye's "Let's Get It On" filled the room, it was on and popping. We stood face to face, titties to titties, anticipating each other's touch.

"Let's take a shower while we're waiting for room service

to get here." Inez led me into the bathroom where we got into the shower and began rubbing soap on each other's bodies until we were both heavily lathered.

"Bend over, Ma. Let me see what you're working with," Inez said.

I complied without hesitation, and Inez began to tongue fuck my tight asshole while at the same time she played with her own clit. Every inch of my body felt like it was on fire. The bitch made me come through my ass. "Oooh, God! Please, don't stop! Yes! Oh, yes!" I screamed as she spread my ass cheeks and buried her long stiff tongue deeper and deeper into my dark tunnel.

By the time room service arrived, we were both laying in bed sharing a two-headed, long and fat, almost human vibrator. The shit was so big and fat that it felt like it was splitting me in half. Inez and I humped our pussies against it until the only thing visible were our clits rubbing against each other.

*"Knock! Knock!"*

"Room service!" a male voice said.

Inez slowly withdrew her half of the vibrator from her pussy with a sloughing sound. Just watching her juicy pussy lips fold back into a tight grip had me cumming. I pulled the vibrator out of me and started sucking on the head that had just come out of her pussy.

Inez opened the door to the suite naked, to find a young boy smiling and holding a tray. "Thank you, sweetie!" she said, and gave the young boy a full view of her body. Her nipples were aiming straight at him like missiles.

"Anything else?" the young boy asked as he stared at me unfazed as I deep throated the vibrator.

"Not right now. I got all I need." Inez grabbed the tray and slammed the door in the young boy's face.

After a few more drinks of vodka with lemon juice, I wanted to show Inez why they called me Sweet Lips. "Lay on your stomach," I instructed her.

Inez quickly complied with my request. Once she lay spread-eagle on the bed, she found herself chatting in breathless, nonstop manners that she couldn't control. Her pussy fluttered. For some reason she couldn't understand what was happening to her body as I continued to suck her toes. A powerful orgasm caused her knees to weaken. Far too soon she opened her eyes and found me looking at her *con una sonrisa de puta.* She was only able to whisper two words, "Don't stop!" I obliged her with more wet kisses.

I crawled in bed between her legs, rubbing the ice cubes down the center of her back until they melted. Inez shivered as the ice cubes sent chills down her spine. I grabbed a pair of thongs and tied Inez's hands to the bed pole. When she tilted her head to the side, I stuck my tongue into her mouth, awakening every nerve in her body. She pushed her ass towards me in desperation. We stared at each other for a few seconds. Then I opened her pussy lips and began inserting ice cubes deep into her pussy, watching in amazement how her hot pussy was dissolving them. I then poured the strawberry ice cream down the crack of her ass and licked it slowly. I let my tongue slide from her split to the clit, and from the butthole to the tailbone. Her heart pounded so hard I thought it would burst out of her chest. A powerful orgasm was building up, one that would leave its recipient begging for mercy.

Inez wasn't sure if she wanted to scream or pass the fuck out. Her mind told her to come and scream, but she couldn't. I kept inserting ice cubes and pouring ice cream down the crack of her ass until she was in tears and begging me to let her come. When I decided she'd had enough, I bit lightly on her clit, allowing her to come. Her body became weak, and after her fourth nut, she passed out.

I had to let shorty know that my pussy game was stronger then hers. I was pleased with my performance, and I'm pretty sure this was a night she wouldn't be able to erase from her mind. I bounced before she awoke. I didn't want her to feel like she was important. This was *my* game, and it was gonna be played *my* way. I wrote her a note and placed it along with my panties on top of the pillow:

> *Dear Inez,*
> *I enjoyed myself last night. Sorry I had to bounce*
> *so early. If it's meant for us to see each other again,*
> *I'm sure we will.*
>
> *P.S. Do you still have any doubts on why they*
> *call me Sweet Lips? I left a small gift for you--smile!*
> **Sincerely, Sweep Lips**

When Inez awoke, her whole body felt numb. Memories of

last night instantly flooded her mind and she got wet between her legs. Her instantaneous attraction to me had been breathtaking, unlike anything she had experienced.

When she got up from bed and looked in the mirror, she couldn't believe her eyes. Her whole body was covered from head to toe with passion marks that looked like small hearts. She smiled, because deep down in her heart, she knew that the script had been flipped. She wouldn't dare admit it to herself, but the bitch was whipped on some next level shit. Whatever ideas she had about turning me out had been squashed, indeed. Now, she'd be forced to endure my form of treatment. I had the advantage over her. She knew nothing about me but my name. On the other hand, I knew everything about her, including her weaknesses, and I sincerely intended to capitalize on them.

# CHAPTER 11
## "A Fair Exchange"

In spite of my determination to get my life back in order, I needed to stay focused on finding my daughter. I decided to walk to Temple Hospital in hopes of seeking some sense of direction.

By the time the receptionist in the records office called my name, I knew she wasn't going to be able to assist me. One thing hasn't changed since I'd been gone, and that was ugly ass bitches hating on good looking women. When the ugly bitch behind the desk looked at me, her whole demeanor switched from, "Good morning, how can I help you?" to "What do you want?"

I remained calm as I approached the desk with a smile. "Hi! My name is Mita Cruz, and I'm seeking information on how to locate my daughter."

"Do you know her name? Is she a patient here?"

"No. She was born in this hospital, but she was put up for adoption by my parents."

The ugly bitch was smirking from ear to ear as if I had said something clever. "That being the case, I can't help you. We're not allowed to reveal any information concerning adoptions. Sorry!" The ugly bitch turned her back towards me and said to another receptionist, "I don't understand why these skank bitches be spreading their legs for these niggas out here, having babies left and right, and then giving them up for adoption. Then they want to come look for them. I'm tired of paying my tax dollars to feed these little crack babies."

I wanted to jump over the counter and bitch slap the shit out this ugly hoe, but years of incarceration had prepared me psychologically to deal with this kind of bullshit. The feelings this disgruntled, ugly hoe had towards me were reciprocated. I took a slow deep breath and walked out of the hospital with a smile. It was time for me to step my game up.

I sat drinking down an orange juice, ear hustling on the conversation the couple was having at the next table in the small cafe across the street from Temple University Hospital. The young Latina smiled and spoke, "...Call me tonight if you're not working. It's been a week since you gave me some." She tilted her head and looked at the young Latino who appeared to be an intern at the hospital.

"I know! I know! But you know how it is. I'm new, so they got me stuck in the records office all day long. Hopefully, once my probation is over, I can start working regular hours. You know I love to be up in your kitten!"

I smiled at the puppy love exchange between the two youngsters. Love is a ma'fucka! I waited until the young girl left before I made my move. I walked over to the young boy's table and said, "You shouldn't be alone in a place like this. My name is Sweet Lips."

The young nigga was startled. "My name is Julio. I'm a

clerk at the hospital."

"What did you say your name was?" I asked again.

"Julio."

"Julio, how long have you been working at the hospital?"

"About three months."

"I see. I've always been fascinated with men who work in hospitals. I believe they don't get treated fairly. I mean, y'all do play a significant role in saving lives."

"You're right. Long hours, little money, lots of problems at home, but it pays the bills though," Julio recited in a sonorous voice.

"Tell me, Julio, are you married? I'll bet a nice looking young man such as you has a lot of girls."

"No, not really. I mean, I have friends, but nothing serious."

"So, are you available?"

"Yeah!"

"Well, listen. I'm new in town. Why don't you take the rest of the day off and show me around the city? I'll make it worth your time."

"Uh… yeah! Why not?" He pulled out his cell phone and made a call. "Ms. Campbell, I got an emergency at home that I must attend to. I won't be in this afternoon."

"Where do we start?" I asked him as I grabbed his arm, and we walked out the cafe as if we were a couple. We walked up and down Germantown Avenue, talking about life issues. But I wasn't trying to spend my day walking with a young boy who looked like a geek in a hospital smock. I wanted him to know that the accommodation lived up to the advertisement. "Julio, have you ever been with an older woman?"

"No."

"Since you don't have to be back at work, why don't you let me show you how much I appreciate your time?" I leaned over and whispered in his ear, "Let me suck your dick. I could make you forget about your little girlfriend. I love to suck dick!" I could see the redness on his cheeks, but my request was too real for him to refuse.

"You don't have to do that... I mean... yeah! But you don't have to."

"I want to. I love to suck dick. Let's go over to your place."

"No. I still live at home with my mother, but we can go to the motel down the block."

*Damn! I got me a mama's boy still wet behind the ears! Fuck it! I need him.* "I'ma only suck your dick. We're not fucking yet."

"I know, I know!"

When we walked into the Sunshine Inn on Germantown Avenue, we received more stares than I'd anticipated. The Sunshine Inn was known throughout North Philly as a dirty, dingy motel for prostitutes. The rooms were dirty and smelled like urine. I didn't mind because I intended on having this young boy busting his gun in no time.

"Strip out of your clothes, sweetie."

He dropped his pants and boxers, and to my surprise, the young nigga was packing nice; maybe 9 to 10 inches in length, with a large purple head. It was real thick with veins popping out from the sides, but it was nothing I couldn't handle.

I had him sit on the edge of the bed while I knelt down between his legs and started sucking his big hairy balls. I wasn't ashamed of getting hair between my teeth. Even though I hadn't sucked a dick in a while, I never lost the touch. While I sucked his balls, I slid my tongue up his butthole. I worked my tongue slowly up his length in circles, then back to his balls, adding a little pressure to my lips. I was leaving passion marks along his length. When pre-cum started pouring out of his dick head, I licked it off.

This young nigga was ready to cry. I smiled when I gave him my signature trademark. I formed my lips into a heart shape and let them rest on his dick head for a second while looking up at him. I detected that he never had his dick sucked this way before. Slowly, I let my lips slide all the way down to his balls, and then back up. I picked up the tempo when I felt his dick vein pausing against my lips. I knew it wouldn't be long before he came. I bobbed my head up and down, left and right, squeezing his balls softly. When I felt he was about to come, I pressed my hot tongue on his pee hole tightly, preventing him from coming.

"Please! Please, let me come!" he begged me.

"Not yet, baby. I don't ever want you to forget these lips. Plus I need--" I went back to bobbing my head up and down slowly.

"You need me to do what?" he asked me while shaking uncontrollably.

"Shhh, be quiet!" When his balls jumped, I bobbed my head up fast, letting him shower my face with his hot cum. I jerked him off slowly until every drop of cum was out, then I licked him clean. Most niggas loved to see their own cum all over a bitch's face. It does something mentally to them.

"Damn, *Mami*! That's the best blow job I ever had!"

"There's more if you act right. I'm glad you loved it. It was my honor. That was just an example of what a real woman can do for you. If you help me, I'll make sure you don't go without sex," I said, while still licking him clean.

"What do you need me to do? Whatever help I can give you, I will."

Now this young nigga was saying something! "You work in the records office at the hospital, and I need you to obtain a copy of all the babies born on September 13, 1990. Can you do that for me, sweetie?"

"Yes, I can, but what's in it for me?"

"Come here, sweetie," I said to him as I lay back on the bed with my legs wide open, holding my pussy lips open with two fingers.

Julio went head first, believing he was gonna eat my shaven pussy. "Taste it! Do you like it?" I pushed his head away, letting him slide a finger in it. "This tight, clean, fat pussy is yours if you get me that list."

Julio's mind was too far gone thinking about my delicious pussy. He would've killed if I'd asked him to. His young girl's pussy was probably sweet, but mine was better and couldn't be compared. "I'll get it for you tomorrow. How do I get in touch with you?" he asked.

"Give me your phone. Whenever you're ready, call your phone, okay?"

"But my girl--"

"Don't worry, the next time she calls I'll let her that now you got a grown woman taking care of you. Now, it's up to you, sweetie."

It didn't take long for Julio to decide. He was sprung. Most niggas got real sensitive about some pussy. They let their weakness dictate their moves. Some good pussy and some incredible head had been the downfall of some of the most powerful men in the world. Look at the ex-governor of New York. A nigga would confess to murder just to get a nut off on a hot chick. Pussy was the oldest game in the world. Niggas were tricks. They would jeopardize their lives and freedom just to impress a chick, and this young lame was no different. He was willing to jeopardize his job for a bitch he'd just met. This was one of the reasons why I hated men with a passion. They always thought with their dicks. Men were some sorry ma'fuckas who deserved all the shit society threw their way--drugs, police ass-whippings, AIDS, jail and death. You can call me a man hater, but fuck it! Twice men had raped me, which entitled me to feel the way I do.

I peeped game a long time ago, and in this diary, you clowns get no play, and fucking with me, niggas are liable to get checked. You see, I was not one of those soft little bitches who suffered from low self-esteem. I was not a broke bitch, nor was I hungry for dick. I was strictly pussy. I got my own paper, and I held a Bachelor's Degree in Business Communications from Penn State University. So I had to spell it out to all those confused niggas: Sweet Lips was the S.H.I.T. I was every nigga's fantasy and every pussy eating, dyke bitch's dream. I loved only me, myself, and I. I could have cared less about how anyone else felt. I got what I wanted, when I wanted it, even if it meant breaking a few nigga's hearts. Soon, this young nigga would learn that an incredible head job would lead to his demise.

# CHAPTER 12
## "Trick Please"

It was close to four weeks after my release when I decided to call Mr. Solomon, the young square from the bank, not because he mattered, but because I found his card in my bag one day, and I was horny and tired of playing with myself. I needed to feel the real thing up in my stomach. A young square like Mr. Solomon exhibited a great level of respect for women when pursuing the pussy. In my book, squares, geeks, hustlers and players got the same treatment. I had made a promise to myself a long time ago that no man would ever take advantage of me, toy with my emotions or view me as a plaything to discard after they fucked me. Those days were long gone. I had a deed that couldn't be buried in the past. I was collecting old debts owed to me by men.

Charles Brightmore once wrote, "A woman must realize knowledge is equal to power. It is therefore essential to discover everything she can about a man, be his friend, enemy or lover. The more she knows, the more power she will be able to wield in the relationship, and the less likelihood that she will be taken advantage of." This was the code I lived by, and it gave me the upper hand when dealing with men.

"Hello, how can I help you?" the soulful voice of a male

vibrated through the phone.

"Can I speak to Mr. Solomon?"

"Speaking. Who's calling?"

"Mita Cruz."

"I know who you are. I've been waiting for your call."

"Really?"

"Yes, really. It's not every day I get to see a beautiful lady in person. Natural beauty is hard to find now a days."

"Are you just gaming me, or is this the charm you give to every woman you meet?"

"Charming, yes. Gaming, no. I gain nothing from playing games. Games are for kids. I'm a grown man with plenty of responsibilities on my shoulders."

"It's good to hear a man speak on responsibilities. That is a word that seems to be missing from their vocabulary, which makes women like me not give men the time of day."

"Well, I'm honored you called me and gave me the time of day and the opportunity. I'm sure as we get to know each other I will demonstrate that I'm a man worthy of your time."

I won't front, this nigga had my panties wet. He didn't even know that he'd been selected the first time I met him to be the third man in my life to ever lay pipe in me. Whether he turned out to be a trusted man or not, he was gonna get this pussy. "Time will tell if you are all rap, or if you are like the other men out here. Until then, I'm going to let my temptations lead the way."

"Good, because my only desire is to make you smile."

"Well, do I get invited to lunch or dinner, or do we just become phone buddies?"

"I have a better idea. Why don't you allow me to show you the city a little. I have some invitations to the City Gala at City Hall on Saturday. Very powerful and influential people gather to raise money for the homeless people in the city. So, will you be my guest?"

"Sure, only if I can bring a friend with me. Being that I'm new in the city, my friend's been my personal tour guide." I threw a monkey wrench in the game just to see if this nigga was after the pussy or not.

"Sure, why not? I will be my honor to play host you and your friend. The dressing attire is formal."

"Well, thank you, but no thanks. Personally, I don't own any evening gown, and I'm on a tight budget. Maybe we could go out another time when the dressing attire is causal."

"I'll tell you what. Since I'm the one who's inviting you, I will see to it that you and your friend are dressed for this event. So why don't you come by the bank tomorrow and pick up my credit card and go shopping?"

This nigga was either stupid or just a generous person. Either way, I intended to use this opportunity to make Inez feel secure. "What time should I come through?"

"I'm in the office all day, until four."

"I'll drop by in the morning."

*"No problema."*

"Oh, so you speak Spanish too!"

"I'm Puerto Rican. What'd you think I was?"

"Honestly, I thought you was black."

"They're our people, too. But what gave you that impression?"

"Your skin completion and your way of speaking. You speak proper English."

"I can get ghetto too."

I laughed out loud, because seriously, I couldn't visualize this nigga acting ghetto. But then again, a book couldn't be judged by its cover. "How so?"

"In due time you'll will find out, but don't let my outside fool you. You can take a nigga out the ghetto, but not the ghetto out of a nigga. I respect the brothers on the corner hustling. At one time I was one of them. I just chose to pursue my dreams of going to college and becoming a financial broker. But I'm 'hood, baby!"

I wasn't impressed by his ghetto background or his sad ass story about making it out of the ghetto. Ever since Obama became president, niggas had been walking around dressing in suits and talking all proper and shit. This nigga was about to blow his chances of having some exclusive pussy, talking all this "I'm ghetto" shit. As soon as I heard Julio's cell phone ring, I knew it was time to cut Mr.-I'm-so-ghetto off. "Listen, I must take care some errands, so I'll see you tomorrow. By the way, what do the brothers in the 'hood call you?"

"Solo."

"So, can I call you Solo?"

"Yes, you may."

"Okay, Solo, I see you *mañana*."

Julio sat in his little cubicle at Temple University Hospital, feeling very much like a cold-blooded sucka. Here he was, risking his dream job for a bitch he only knew as Sweet Lips. He glanced around the room and felt like he was being watched. Guilt and regret catapulted to the surface, but the thought of being able to get his dick sucked by a hot chick made him ignore his breach of security at the hospital.

I had been the first woman to ever suck his dick, and the second woman he'd ever been with. After a brief hesitation, Julio decided to dial my number again. Although I missed his last two calls, I knew he would call again, so I wasn't sweating it. In fact, it gave me more time to focus on my game plan. When Julio called again, I smiled because he was probably wondering if he'd been played. I let his phone ring for a good five minutes. I wanted him to realize that he should be more careful with what he wished for, as he might just get it. When I decided to answer, I added a whiff of sarcasm to my voice. "I know your not blowing up this phone for nothing!"

"Who's this?"

"Who this? I'm the bitch who sucked your dick like none other bitch has!"

"Excuse me!" a female voice said, almost in a whisper.

"Let me guess. You are Julio's girlfriend, right?"

"Yes, I am, and who the fuck are you? And what are you doing with Julio's phone?"

"Like I said, I'm the bitch who's been sucking his dick like you never done before. If you don't believe me, inspect his dick and you will see my lip prints on it."

She winced. "You are lying!"

"If you say so, child, but do me and you a favor. Don't call Julio any more, 'cause once I get done with him, your dumb young ass will be history. My advice to you is, learn how to suck a dick while you're still young. Have a nice day!" I outright cut this little heifer off because she wasn't in my league.

When the phone rang again, I thought it was her again, but this time it was a male voice. "Wassup, Ma? I been calling you for almost a week now."

"Wassup, Ma! First of all, I'm not your ma, and second, I'm about to throw this phone away if you don't start talking to me like you got some fucking sense!" I said. I wanted this young lame to feel like I was doing him a favor by letting him call me on his own phone.

"I was just joking with you. I'm sorry."

This lame was pure pussy. If it weren't because I needed him, I wouldn't have given him the time of day. "You got what I asked you for?"

"Yes, I do. That's why I'm calling."

"So, when can we meet?"

"I have to work tomorrow. How about Saturday afternoon?"

"Cool! I'll meet you at the cafe where we first met. I got a surprise for you."

"The only surprise I want is a shot of pussy. I've been thinking about you all week. I think I'm--"

This young lame had the game twisted. His words had proven to me that he'd attached far too much significance to a meaningless head job. Damn! I knew I had a helluva head game, but it was obvious this young lame had blown the entire episode out of proportion. "You are aware that sex is the normal compensation for your services?"

"That's all I'm looking for."

Conversing with this young supercilious lame turned my stomach. Clearly something about men never changed. The hollow ache in my gut indicated that perhaps it was time for me to start checking niggas on some real shit. Some men were perfectly content living and thinking with their dicks, and this young lame wasn't any different. I was pretty sure he never suspected the ordeal that awaited him fucking with a bitch like me. "I'm more than glad to be able to service you, sweetie. See you on Saturday."

His mama should've told him to be careful with what he wished for, because his wishes might come true.

Once my plans were in motion, I decided to call Inez. I deliberately had her ass on pause ever since that first night when we fucked. I wanted her to feel less than what she really thought she was. It was my own little way of showing her who was in control. I was willing to bet she was suffering withdrawal symptoms. The little bitch was a nympho, and no one had to tell me I was the best she's ever had. I wanted to keep her in rampant paranoia.

"Hello?"

I smiled when I heard her voice. I could tell I was the source of her discomfort. "Can I speak to Inez?"

"Speaking... oh my God! I didn't recognize your voice! Why haven't you called me?" she asked.

"I'm calling now. I was busy."

"When can I see you again?"

"I don't know. I'm busy."

"Busy!"

I could hear an attitude in her voice and I was unruffled by her sassy tone.

"If you're busy, why are you calling now?"

"Just checking up on you. Maybe it's the wrong time, huh?"

"No! I just want to see you again."

"You will."

"When?"

"I don't know!" I decided to play with her for a while to see how far she was willing to go. "Inez, right now you are sounding like a thirsty bitch. I was under the impression that our little tryst was a one-night thing, but you're acting like you my wifey and shit. Wassup with that?"

"I don't mean to sound like a thirsty bitch, but I'm feeling you and I'm willing to do whatever it takes to be a part of your world, no strings attached. I could be your wifey, lover and best friend. I'm a ride or die kind of chick, straight up!"

"You know that being my wifey comes with some rules?"

"I'm loyal. Death before dishonor."

"Are you just talking out of emotions, or are you talking from the heart?"

"From the heart. Ever since I first laid eyes on you, I knew I wanted to be a part of your world," she said with confidence.

"Let me put it this way to you, mama! Sex is just something I enjoy, but my life consists of other things. I don't have time to baby-sit or cater to anyone's needs. I'm at a point in life where it's all about me. If you want to be part of my world, you must be ready for whatever." I was making sure she was receiving the message that was being delivered: My game, my rules, or keep it moving.

"I'm ready!"

"Are you sure? Because once we cross that line there's no turning back, there's no excuses, ifs, ands or buts. Your pussy will be off limits to everyone else. I don't share pussy. You think you're ready for that kind of relationship?" My words seemed to linger in her ears, resonating unspoken possibilities.

"It's all about you, Ma. I'm ready."

"A'ight!"

"So, are we official, or what? Because I'm ready to move you into my place."

I was loving her spunk. "Let's meet up first and talk about our plans for each other. One step at a time, okay?"

"Whatever you say, boss lady!"

"By the way, shave your pussy up for me."

"I have a better idea. Why don't you do it when we get together?"

"My honor, *Mami!*"

"So, when do we get together?"

"What are you doing now?"

"Laying in bed thinking of you. Why?"

"Come pick me up, same place you did the first time, in ten minutes." I had no intention of giving up my little place to move in with Inez. Just in case things between us didn't work out, I still had a place to lay my head at night. All the pieces to my plan were finally coming together.

Unmistakable recognition flashed in Inez's eyes when she saw me waiting for her in front of the Painted Bride Art Center with my Frankie B. Jeans and Versace stilettos. There was no mistaking who was in charge. Inez was certain she did the right thing by opening her heart to me. For a brief moment, I lusted for my young trophy, almost forgetting my agenda. At the moment I had the upper hand in this game, and I intended to play it like a chess game, checking the King and ensuring it was forced to checkmate before it regrouped and went on the defense. I needed her on my team to do my dirty work in the name of love.

Our eyes met for a moment as she got out of the car, her hair covering one side of her face as her kitten rubbed against the hem of her jeans. "Wassup, Ma?" she crooned, sliding her tongue inside my mouth. We cradled against each other in public like an official couple.

"You act as you if you're been missing me forever," I said with a laugh.

For an answer, Inez grabbed my hand and guided it towards her pussy and whispered in my ear, "I can't wait until you shave all this hair off!" She nibbled on my ear lob.

"Tonight, baby. First we got to handle some business."

Inez nodded slowly. "Such as?"

"Personal business! I told you earlier that if you going to ride with me, you must be down for whatever. So, are you down for running game on niggas?"

"For you, I'll do anything. However, I thought you said you don't share pussy."

"I don't. I ain't say shit about sharing pussy. I asked you a simple question. Are you down for running game on niggas?" I repeated again, looking Inez straight in the eyes.

"Are you testing me? I told you I'm a ride or die chick."

"Good. Because on Saturday we have a full day," I replied, chuckling.

"What are the plans?" Inez asked, interrupting my thoughts.

"I have two corny niggas lined up for the takedown. One works at Temple Hospital, the other one is a banker with a taste for some sweet lips, willing to send us on a shopping spree tomorrow. We deal with him on Saturday night. The clown from the hospital is the one we need to focus on at this point. He has the list of all the babies born on the date my daughter was born. He thinks he's going to get some pussy, but I have a big surprise

for him. Make sure you bring some of your toys for this date."

"You crazy as hell!" Inez said.

"You haven't seen crazy yet."

We spent the rest of the day laid up in Inez's bed, taking turns eating each other's assholes clean. I won't front, this young girl's pussy smelled like roses.

"Ma, my pussy itches a little. It feels funny not having any hair down there."

"You'll get used to it, trust me," I said, sliding my tongue up and down her slit.

"Wow! I'm cummin'! I'm cummin' for you, Ma!"

By nine o'clock Friday morning, Inez and I were at the bank waiting to be escorted into Mr.-I-could-get-ghetto's office. Ten minutes later, he came out of his office smiling from ear to ear. "Ladies! I'm sorry for keeping y'all waiting. I was caught up in an early morning meeting with my staff. I'm glad y'all waited." He looked at me and then at Inez and asked, "Are you two related?"

"I'm sorry, let me introduce you two. Inez, this is Solo. Solo, this is Inez. No we are not related. Inez is my girlfriend," I said, studying his demeanor.

"I heard nice things about you, Solo. I'm looking forward to peeking into your mind for some wisdom on banks, so thank you kindly for the invitation." Inez had the nigga dizzy, and he didn't even try to hide his hard on.

"I'm sure tomorrow will be special for us three. It gives

me much pleasure knowing I'll be in the company of two of the most beautiful ladies in Philadelphia." Solo handed me his credit card and told me not to worry about the spending limit. I smiled, because my intentions were to treat Inez and myself to the best outfits a trick's money could buy. I inspected the credit card for a brief moment and noticed it didn't have his name on it. Instead, it had the bank's name, which could only mean that this nigga was tricking with the bank's credit card.

"Well, Solo, where should we meet up tomorrow? And what time does this event start?" I asked, feeling disgusted. This nigga was standing in front of me with a hard on, looking at Inez as if he wanted to fuck her on the spot, and I was feeling a little jealous.

"Call me at 6:30 p.m. and I'll send a car over to pick y'all up."

"Okay, Solo. I guess we'd better get going." Inez and I both winked at him as we walked out of the bank with a piece of plastic that was worth more money than either one of us had ever seen.

"Ma! You see his hard on? That's why I can't stand men!" Inez said, making it clear to me that she was only playing her part.

"Yeah, I saw him. His stupid ass don't even realize how disrespectful that move was. But what can a bitch expect from a man? I'm sure this would ease the pain," I said, waving the credit card in her face.

"He probably believes he's gonna fuck us both. I'm willing

to bet he probably can't handle one of us. He definitely has ulterior motives," Inez said.

Inez and I were minding our business shopping at the Sak's Boutique in Center City, when a guy approached us. "Excuse me; I will pay for your order if you allow me a minute of your time."

I instantly recognized the voice, but decided to ignore it. "No, thanks, I pay for my own shit," I said with a slight attitude.

"I got a thousand dollars for some conversation." Suso was persistent in his quest for conversation, and I was getting frustrated.

"Sometimes you got to know when to stop begging, young boy. It makes you look desperate."

Suso's eyebrows rose as if I was saying something wrong. I found it fascinating to see the length a nigga goes to for some attention. With a disgusted exclamation, he grabbed my arm, which instantly enraged me.

"Nigga, get your hands off me!"

"Oh! My money ain't good? Not long ago my money was good! Fuck you, bitch! I should just fuck you in the ass right here on GP!" he said. His expression was unreadable. I couldn't believe this punk ass nigga was actually threatening to rape me. I remained calm.

"You got about two seconds before I make you regret your actions!" Inez said as she held her 9-mm under his balls.

Suso's eyes were heated with hate. "You ain't that crazy to shoot me inside a store full of people," he said.

"Test me if you want, you pretty ma'thafucka, and watch me turn you into a faggot, because after I blow your nuts off, the only thing you're going to be able to do is take it in the ass, nigga! I'm finished with these games!"

Suso was so caught up in the moment that he failed to realize Inez had a silencer on her gun, and that we were in the back of the dressing room of the store with no one in sight. Something flashed in his eyes. He dropped to his knees. The burning sensation in his nut sack was unbearable. Before he could muster enough energy to let out a bitch ass scream, Inez pressed the heel of her stiletto into his throat, crushing his windpipe.

"Look at you now, you pretty ma'thafucka!" Inez said, pumping one hot pill in the top of his melon. "A dead nigga can't talk. This punk nigga could've definitely identified us. I'm not trying to go to prison," she said as if she was trying to justify her actions to me.

"Damn, baby! I had no idea you harbored such violent tendencies!"

"I told you I'm a ride or die chick."

Inez and I walked out of Sak's with two beautiful gowns and a secret we both promised to carry to our graves. We ended up spending close to thirty-five thousand dollars. Versace, Frankie B. Ralph Lauren, Zac Posen, Channel, Salvatore Farragora and Gucci all graced our shopping bags. With the recession at its peek, I felt like a little white bitch in Beverly Hills. We did exactly what Solo instructed us to do--shop until we got tired.

Saturday morning was promising to be a good one. I awoke to the smell of frying bacon, fried eggs, cinnamon toast, orange juice, cheese bagels and coffee. "Breakfast, huh?" I said. "You need help?"

"Nah. My treat, baby. It's Saturday, breakfast in bed," Inez said in breathy pants, her chest heaving.

"I feel special. This is very kind of you."

"You are special," Inez said. "Lay back and enjoy my cooking."

Breakfast. Inez served it with candles around the food tray, creating a romantic atmosphere. "I'd like to thank you, Inez, for breakfast... for what you did yesterday."

"I told you I'm a ride or die chick, Ma." Inez buried her head under the sheets, treating herself to an early morning desert.

"Daaamn! That's the spot, baby!" I gripped her head tight, rubbing my *toto* (pussy) against her magical lips.

We arrived at Temple Cafe ten minutes early, and to our surprise, Julio was already there. "Got-damn! You never told me you had a twin sister!" he said when he saw Inez standing next to me.

"Yup! And if you got what I asked you for, maybe we will treat you to every man's dream." Inez and I both gave him an engaging eye, making him feel like he was the man.

"I got what you requested over at my mother's crib. She's out of town, so we can chill over there," Julio said, grabbing his dick in his hands.

We drove to his crib in a beat up black Honda Accord. Inez left her car parked in front of Temple Hospital to avoid any unnecessary suspicion. Julio's mother lived down on Mole Street near Morris Street, in a two story house tucked in the corner of a dead end street. I observed the block as I got out of the car, and with the exception of one or two fiends, the block was empty,

"Ladies, we got the house all to ourselves for a few days if we want," Julio said nonchalantly as we entered the house.

Inez and I looked at each other as if to say, this nigga must be out of his mind!

"I don't know about a few days, but we definitely are going to treat you to something real nice after we handle our business," I said as I gave him a seductive stare while licking my fingers.

"Here is all I could find, all the dates of birth of all the babies born on September 13, 1990. The computer doesn't provide names. However, I did manage to get the name of the agency that did the adoption transaction for the hospital at that time. That should be enough to lead you in the right direction. I told you I got you." Julio tossed an envelope on top of the table. When I reached for the envelope, he pushed my hand away and said, "You get it after I get the surprise you said you got for me."

"What, you don't trust me?"

"It's not personal, it's business, nah-mean?"

I guess this punk ass nigga felt safe because we were inside his house, but soon he would regret the audacity it took to put his hands on me. My entire demeanor changed, but I remained calm even though I was fuming inside. "A'ight."

"A'ight my ass! Both of you skanks better start dropping them panties! I want some pussy!"

I knew for sure now that this nigga must'a bumped his head somewhere, or he was high, talking to me from the side of his neck like he was crazy. "Are you serious?"

"I'm dead serious, hooker! You want this?" He waved the envelope. I couldn't fully decipher who could've ruffled this asshole's feathers. His eyes flicked towards Inez, who had already taken her shirt and sweatpants off, giving him a view of that big ass she was carrying.

"I'm first! I want me some of that dick. I want you to blow my back out first. I want you to fuck me in the ass," Inez said, pulling his dick out of his pants and rubbing her hand up and down on it.

"Let's go to my mom's bedroom. She has a king size bed we can all fit in." Julio was drooling all over himself.

Once inside the bedroom, I smiled because it appeared that Julio's mom had been getting her freak on. Porn movies lay out in the open, vibrators on top of the nightstand, and used condoms left on the side of the bed. Not only was his mom a freak, she was a dirty freak at that.

"You ready for your surprise?" I asked him while I crawled into the bed and started playing with his balls. Inez peeked the move and wrapped her lips around his hard dick. I knew this nigga must have thought he had died and gone to heaven, because he closed his eyes, threw his hands behind his head and moaned like a little bitch. When Inez had him ready to come, I bit down on one of his balls with all my might until I heard it pop like a grape nut. Inez quickly reached into her bag and pulled out a pair of handcuffs and cuffed his ass to the bed, then quickly dressed.

When this young nigga came to, his bloodshot, teary eyes told a different story from the one he was telling earlier. "Come on, baby! I thought we had a deal!" he managed to say, closing his eyes shut as if that was supposed to alleviate the pain.

"We did have a deal until you started acting funny, talking crazy to us! Now the deal is off, and I still get what I came for!"

"I was only playing! I'm not a bad person! I was only playing!" Julio started to cry. "I was only playing... please don't hurt me! I promise I won't tell anyone!"

"You're making me blush!" I laughed out loud.

"Man-up, nigga! Don't cry now!" Inez's adrenaline rush was running high as she grabbed a vibrator from on top of his mother's dresser and started inserting it up Julio's ass and turning on the switch.

"You must sacrifice your asshole now for all the shit you was talking!" I whispered in his ear as I wrapped a plastic shopping bag around his neck, securing it tightly with duct tape.

"Let's get the fuck out of here," I told Inez as I gathered the remaining duct tape, the envelope and Inez's panties and threw them inside Inez's bag.

Inez wiped down everything we touched. Before we left the room, she poured a bottle of alcohol on top of Julio, who was struggling to catch his breath. Afterwards, she lit a candle that Julio's mom had on top of the dresser and threw it on the bed next to him.

We walked out of the house calmly. Once outside, I lit a match and threw it inside the gasoline tank of Julio's beat up car. Inez and I left the crime scene without a trace.

At four o'clock, while in Inez's house preparing for our date with Solo, Fox News flashed scenes of a burnt house on Mole Street. Inez and I both looked at each other and smiled.

*"Breaking News! Philadelphia police are investigating what has been described as a bizarre and tragic crime. Police believe that a young man role playing with a dominatrix may have caused his own death. No foul play is suspected. They are looking to speak with two white women who they consider people of interest. The victim's mother, Nancy Smith Brown, described her son as a good young man with a promising career in the medical field. He was an intern at Temple University Hospital. Officials at the hospital tell us the victim was a hard working young man. The victim's girlfriend, not believed to be a person of interest, informed us that she is six weeks pregnant. This is Linda Hart, reporting live for Fox 29 News."*

The cameraman held a still shot of Julio's mother hugging what appeared to be his girlfriend. It only took a second for me to recognize Julio's mother's face. *Damn, Nancy! I didn't know that was your son! Fuck it!* If she was my best friend like

I thought she was, she would'a stayed in contact with me when I was serving my time. She should'a sent me some flicks of her family, but she forgot about me like everyone else did, so I have no remorse for her loss.

# CHAPTER 13

## "Behind Closed Doors"

Inez, Solo and I arrived in a stretch Limousine in front of City Hall to attend the fund raiser gala for the city's homeless. We both had revealed to Solo the fact that neither one of us were wearing any panties under our Oscar De La Renta dresses. From inside the Limo, we could see the line of European cars dropping off the city's most influential people.

The red carpet was packed with the city's media and groupies who were trying to catch a crooked politician. All the heavy hitters in the city were in attendance. Senator Vince Fumo, who'd recently been convicted for embezzlement, Governor Rendell, Mayor Nutter, Jada and Will Smith, The Roots, Jill Scott, Charlie Mack, Eric Heart, and Eve. Philadelphia's beloved daughter, Miss Patti LaBelle, was the special guest of the event.

Solo was grinning from ear to ear as all eyes were on him when we entered the reception room. There was no fronting, we were stunning. All the middle aged, worn out bitches were staring at us with pure hatred in their eyes.

After Solo, Inez and I made our way through the crowd, we ended up sitting next to the Governor, who appeared to be trying to convince anyone who would listen that Vince Fumo was innocent. Apparently Solo felt like he was in his element, because he greeted everyone he thought was someone of power. I mean, I knew this clown wasn't the hard core type of nigga who could hold water if push came to shove, but to see him trying to break his neck just to rub elbows with a bunch of white men was ridiculous. Malcolm X, Martin Luther King and all the black legends who had fought for equality were probably turning over in their graves knowing Solo was the type of nigga their struggle had produced.

"Solo, we'll be right back," I said, as Inez and I got up from our plush chairs and headed towards the bar.

"Girl, I'm glad we broke away from that tap dancing nigga. He acts like he wants to suck the Governor's dick. He's worse than a groupie," Inez said, and then ordered two glasses of Krug Rose from the pale faced bartender.

"Yeah. Niggas are always looking to impress the white man by playing stupid, as if that's supposed to help them climb the ladder of success. They kill me with--"

"Inez!" An older white man called out, rubbing his hands across her shoulders. "Long time don't see, young lady."

Inez forced a smile and placed a kiss on the man's cheek. "Hi, Judge. I'm glad you are here supporting this noble cause. How've you been?"

"I could be better if my favorite girl would call me from time to time. Who's the beautiful young lady with you?"

"Oh, she's my best friend, Sweet Lips. She's new in the city."

The judge looked me over as if he knew me from somewhere. His eyes still had the same perverted look as they had the day he sentenced me to prison. What a small world!

"Well, young lady, why don't you call me on Monday morning so we can arrange lunch? It would be my honor to treat two beautiful ladies," the judge said while looking at my cleavage.

"I promise I'll call you," Inez said.

The Judge turned towards me and rubbed my breast slightly, and then said, "It was a pleasure meeting you, Miss Sweet Lips."

I nodded my head, even though I wanted to slap the shit out of him for touching my breast. But I didn't want to create a scene in front of the people, who in the future may be able to help me in my quest to find my daughter. "Who the fuck was that, Inez?"

"He's a City Judge. He's a freak. He loves to be tied up and whipped. He's the one who bought me my car. Every once in a while I go over his to chambers, piss in his mouth, spank him, then charge him up. He likes wearing women's clothes." Inez had more skeletons in the closet than I thought, but I admired her hustle and honesty. She was about that paper, and what better way to get it than from these freak ass influential crooked politicians?

"You definitely got to put me up on him."

"That goes without saying. We're partners so there's plenty for both of us." We both laughed out loud.

*"I fuck rich powerful men for money."* Those were Inez's words on our first date. Now I was really grasping the true

meaning of those words. I wondered how many of the rich and powerful men in the room Inez had fucked. I wasn't even jealous because I'm not one to hate on a bitch's hustle. It could only be beneficial to me. I just had to make sure I kept Inez on a tight leash.

"I suppose you want to know how I know most of these people in here," Inez said with a smile.

"I can not deny it, I am curious, but what I actually wonder is who else besides the Judge in here are you fucking?"

After several minutes of silence, Inez said, "You will be surprised, but fifty percent of the time, fucking ain't got nothing to do with it. Most of these men up in here just want to be around someone who allows them to express themselves, like your boy, Solo--"

"I'm particularly eager to hear it," I responded.

"Your boy, Solo, he loves pussy, but he also loves to act like a punk. He acts all hard, but he is pure pussy. You will see tonight," Inez said with a serious face.

My stomach churned with disbelief. Every negative emotion I felt towards men--anger, contempt, hatred and loathing--boiled up and flooded over.

"Ladies, I'm ready to get out of here. My place is not far from here," Solo said.

"We're ready when you're ready, *Papi*," Inez said.

I couldn't take my eyes off of Solo.

The after-party took place at Solo's condo. His condo was elegant, with a pretty balcony looking directly at Ben Franklin on top of City Hall. The place had other odds and ends that many people with money consider necessary to be happy. For a single man's pad, the place had the touch of a female.

"Can I use your bathroom?" I asked Solo. I wanted to check out the layout of the place in hopes of finding something that would indicate who this nigga really was, but the bathroom was neat. As soon as I returned from the bathroom, I overheard Solo say, "Does she know about us, Inez?"

"Solo, stop panicking. She's cool. Trust me, she's got the best pussy in town, but she's off limits to the dick. You got to respect that."

"Fuck that! I'ma wet my dick tonight. She's gonna to break me off with a shot. All that money y'all spent yesterday should cover the tab."

"If she wants to fuck you, she will, but you are not bullying your way into the pussy, That's real rap. Let her decide what she wants."

I wanted to beat the shit out of him. Instead, I took a deep breath. Inez was on the floor sucking Solo's dick deep into her mouth. I took my cell phone out of my bag and started snapping pictures of him. After he came all over Inez's face, he knelt down next to her and licked his own cum off her face. "Damn, baby! I wish I was double-jointed so I could suck my own dick!" he said.

"What? I'm not enough for you?" Inez asked.

"Yeah, but I just like the way my own cum tastes. I'm ready for some pussy now."

I stormed into the living room as if I wasn't aware of what was happening. "I see y'all started without me, huh?"

"Naw, we were just waiting on you, baby," Solo said, holding his dick in his hand. The nigga was large.

I let my dress slide off my body, and then lay on my back with my legs wide open. Solo wrapped a condom around his dick and threw one of my legs over his shoulder, slowly sliding his dick into my pussy. After the first seven inches were in, he realized my shit was super tight. With every push forward, he was discovering untouched territory. When all twelve inches were buried balls-deep, I began throwing the pussy at him. I felt like I was being split in half. His heavy nut sack was tickling my asshole.

Out of the corner of my eyes I saw Inez strap on one of the longest dildos I had ever seen, and she started pounding Solo's asshole out the farm. Baby girl was fucking this nigga's asshole like a nigga does his woman when he comes home from prison.

I came after the first twenty strokes. When Solo pulled out of me, Inez still had the dildo buried inside him. He took off the condom he was wearing and started swallowing his own cum.

Inez pulled out of him, and goddamn, she had at least eighteen inches of plastic dick up in him. He lay on his back like a little bitch and wrapped his lips around the dildo, treating himself to a mouth full of his own shit. Inez winked at me as I took out my cell phone again and started snapping more pictures. Inez then took the credit card that we had used the day before and slid it between this punk's ass cheeks.

"Ugh, that's crazy!" I said to Inez, referring to how freaky

Solo was. It's funny how these Homo ass niggas out here are into pussy, but at the same time they want their assholes blown out.

"I told you he was a punk."

"Yes, you did. I'm just mad that all that dick is going to waste. I gave him a shot of pussy thinking he was going to tear the pussy up, but all he did was taste me. I'm still horny."

"Don't worry, baby, I'll take care of you when we get over to my place." Inez was a young girl, but she was a beast in the bedroom. She handled my pussy better than any nigga with a dick. All my sexual encounters had been nothing but disappointments and let downs. It's a shame I had to turn to another woman for some real satisfaction.

# CHAPTER 14

### "Fringe Benefits"

I left Inez's house early the next morning, with a determined plan in mind. I still wasn't comfortable with lettering her know where I lay my head at night. Shit had been jumping of so quickly that I needed to re-evaluate my plans for her. I underestimated her, and time after time she was stepping up to the plate, demonstrating her loyalty to me.

I spent the entire morning and afternoon carefully inspecting the contents of the envelope I took from, Julio's house. I tapped my lips with my fingers as I re-read the papers with a speculative look in my eyes. There had been twelve babies delivered on September 13, 1990, and only four of them were put up for adoption. One of those babies had to be mine. Julio even attached the name of the agency that had handled the adoptions.

Tears flowed freely down my face as I thought of seeing my daughter for the first time. I sat up in bed and decided to write my daughter a letter. Maybe one day I'd get the chance to give her the letter personally.

> *Baby girl,*
> *I understand that you may have doubts, and*

*you are probably frustrated, and I'm very sorry or the way you feel and for how things between us ended. The truth of the matter is I never had a say-so in putting you up for adoption. Your grandmother, my mother, took the liberty to do that herself. I have been thinking about you since the day you were born. I always loved you, and never will stop. As long as I have one ounce of breath in me, I will never stop searching for you. When I walk the streets, I look at the faces of all the beautiful young ladies and ask myself, could you be one of them? Who knows? Perhaps we have passed by each other and didn't even know it.*

*From time to time, I feel like you're near me. I feel you calling me, but when I turn around and look, I see no one. I know you have plenty of questions, and I want to answer them one day. A mother-to-daughter heart-to-heart conversation will answer a lot of your questions, and give you an understanding on why it took me so long to begin my search for you.*

*Mrs. Penny, your real grandmother, the lady who took care of me, was in the process of trying to adopt you, but she suddenly died. Now it's you and me against the world.*

*Baby, it's not your fault you were put up for adoption. You did nothing wrong, always remember that. I will always have your back until the casket drops. For nineteen years, life's been a constant pain. I'm sorry my no good mother wreaked so much havoc on us. This may not be much, but it's the least I can do, and that's to provide you with an accurate account of what really happened and the reason for our separation.*

*I love you, baby, and I promise that one day we will find each other.*

*Love,*
*Your Mother*

When I was finished writing the letter, the tears subsided leaving me shaking and weak-kneed. I lay back in bed, and after I re-read the letter, I had to admit that I was feeling much better. I retrieved the papers I took from Julio's house and circled the names I wanted to investigate first. I fell asleep thinking of my daughter, wondering if she was thinking of me.

I awoke in the middle of the night sweating. Loneliness had overtaken me. I was having a hell of a time trying to sleep. I had become accustomed to being in Inez's bed. The memory of Rafael fucking my brains out came swiftly, along with the lessons he had taught me. By the time I was ready to confront the world on my own, I was prepared to survive and show society that I didn't need a man to do shit for me. I had paid dearly with my innocence and didn't have any regrets.

The urge to call Inez was almost irresistible. The walls of

my bedroom were closing in on me. While the need to feel her next to me was strong, I wasn't as strong as I appeared to be. I was strung out on her, and so was she... she was in love. I tossed and turned from side to side, trying to find a comfortable position. My nudity tangled with the sheets, and my pussy ached.

I rolled over and sat on the edge of the bed, and picked up the urban novel, "Trife Life 2 Lavish" by my favorite author, Deja King. I hammered a pillow into a lump, and then placed it between my legs. After hours of reading, I managed to get out of bed and head for the shower. By the time I was done, day was beginning to break, and I once again anticipated seeing Inez.

It was 8:30 in the morning; I was already dressed in a white Fendi sweatsuit, anticipating Inez's call. I knew she was gonna call me, but if she didn't, fuck It! I had a few things to handle anyway.

All kinds of things were running through my mind. The way I figured it, Inez had proven to me that she was down for me. But was it smart to keep her around? Hell, yeah! There was no greater feeling than the rush I got knowing that I had a bitch who would do anything for me. This was the ultimate rush. It was like I was a god to her. What could match that feeling? Inez was hooked on my pussy like a junkie looking for a hit, and I was the only dope bitch in town who could contain her. Determination counted for a lot. Inez was determined to win my heart, even if it meant committing murder, as if that would balance things out. Mentally, psychologically and physically, I knew how she functioned, which gave me the upper hand. I had this young bitch at my disposal, like a puppet on a string.

"Shit! I didn't want to appear desperate, but I needed to hear her voice." My words seemed to echo off my bedroom walls. I couldn't even front. I had no control over my reaction towards her. No nigga or bitch alike had never made me feel this way, or affected me so powerfully. True indeed, I had to get my early morning dose of Sweet Lips. Appearing desperate was the least of my concerns. I picked up my cell phone and pressed the speed dial button. She picked up the phone on the first ring.

"Good morning, baby!"

Inez's voice instantly caused my pussy to jump against my panties.

"Did you sleep well last night?" she asked me in a whisper.

"No, not really."

"Why not?"

"Because I miss you, baby." I was fucking with this young bitch's mind.

"So why don't you move into my crib? That way you won't have to miss me."

There was a long pause. I could hear Inez breathing through the phone. I waited a few more moments before I spoke again. "Don't you think we're moving too fast? I mean, I'm feeling your vibe. I appreciate your company, but moving in together is a major step."

"You know where my heart lays. My loyalty belongs to you. My heart is in your hands. I don't play games when it comes to love. Right now, love is what I feel for you, Ma. I want to wake up in the morning next to you. I want to be able to make love to you every night. I want to be able to touch you and hold you at night."

Silence seemed to fall in rhythm with my own heartbeat. My job was to explore this young chick's weaknesses. Before I could think of a suitable reply, Inez said, "Why are you so afraid for me to love you, Ma? Are you underestimating my loyalty towards you?"

"Naw, I just never lived with anyone before. I always lived on my own."

"There's a first time for everything."

"Why me?"

"Why not?"

"Because there are a lot of things you don't know about me. I'm not your typical lesbian looking for a come-up, I'm high-maintenance."

"And?"

"And if you ain't ready to dance to my tune, it's best that you keep it moving while you are ahead of the game." I wanted to laugh out loud because this bitch was right where I wanted her. Instead, I found myself fascinated. I was eager to hear what she would say next.

"I'm pledging my life to you because I'm digging your style, flow and swagger. I appreciate natural beauty."

"Would you still feel my style, flow and swagger if I was a fat bum bitch?"

"You're making it sound like I'm wrong for wanting to spend my life with a beautiful lady."

"Not at all. I'm just making sure you're not blinded by lust, 'cause if we're gonna commit to each other, I expect honor and integrity." The plan was to make myself unforgettable to her. If I decided to move in with her, I was going to make certain that it was on my own terms.

"Haven't I proven my sincerity to you yet?"

"Yes, you have."

"So?"

"So, if I move in with you, you're gonna have to respect my space, the same way I will respect yours."

She swallowed and said, "I have a feeling we're going to get along very well."

"I'll be at your place tomorrow with my things, unless you want me to come by your job and pick up the keys."

"No, I'll be here. I took two weeks of my vacation time, so you can stop by today if you want to," Inez said.

There was no time to be on some lovey-dovey shit, so I immediately cut into her thoughts. "Listen, did you arrange for us to have lunch with the Judge?"

"Yes, my lady! We are on for tomorrow afternoon in his chambers. He's probably gonna want some freak shit done to him." She cleared her throat and then asked, "Why are you so interested in the Judge, anyway?"

"I'd rather answer that question in person. Let's just say he's a blast from my past-- someone who owes me a lot." I took an exaggerated breath.

"Huh? But--"

"I'll talk to you in person, okay? I'll be over about three o'clock."

"Why so late?"

"Because I got to handle some business."

"Anything I can assist you with?"

"No, not right now."

"Okay, I'll see you at three then."

"By the way, make sure the kitten is clean. I'm trying to eat as soon as I get there."

"I'm ready, Ma!" Inez's voice came out in a weak squeak.

It was only 9:15 a.m. when I got off the phone with Inez, and I decided to go to the cemetery and pay Mrs. Penny a visit. I've never been to a cemetery before, but this was something I had to do. In fact, it's the least I could do for the lady who practically saved my life.

When I arrived at the Holy Sepulchre Cemetery in Cheltenham, it took me half an hour to locate her gravesite. When the caretaker located it for me, I looked at it and stared at the tombstone with tears in my eyes. I sat next to her tombstone for a while before I spoke.

"I'm sorry, Mrs. Penny, for not visiting you sooner. I've been home for a few months now, and life is beautiful. I wouldn't trade it for anything. I won't lie to you, I'm still lonely, but I'm surviving. Remember, I promised you that I would find my daughter. I'm working on that right now. It's not as easy as I thought, but I'm not giving up."

"I did meet a beautiful young lady who's been keeping me company. I know you don't agree with my choices or life style, but I'm not sure I could ever trust another man ever again. You always begged me to forgive those who did harm to me. Mrs. Penny, I haven't been able to do that yet."

"Mrs. Penny, I love you, and I promise I will come visit you every week, just like you visited me in prison. Next time I'll bring you the carnation flowers you like. Maybe I'll bring Inez, my girlfriend, so you can meet her…"

I spent four hours sitting and talking to Mrs. Penny. It almost felt like the first time she took me into her house from the soup line, and when she took care of me throughout my pregnancy. I cried, smiled, and wondered why the only person I ever loved had to die on me.

"…Mrs. Penny, I'll see you next week, and I promise that when I find my baby, I'll will bring her to meet her real grandmother. Smile, my angel! I'm spending the money you left me wisely. I love you!"

Before I left the cemetery, I had to visit two more gravesites. It was about a mile from Mrs. Penny's gravesite in the poorest section of the cemetery where they bury the homeless and unidentified bodies. At the bottom of a hill and far away from the view of any visitors, buried underneath some unattended bushes, two yellow crosses sat tilted to the side, with Sonia and

Rafael's names on them. Even in death, these two junkies were kept away from the public.

"Mom, I know you are surprised to see me here, but you shouldn't be, because I'm not like you. I'm only here so you can see how beautiful I am. Even though you abused me, allowed Rafael to rape me, and sold me out for crack money, I'm still standing and still surviving. I'm also laughing because you can't hurt me any more. Life is beautiful, and believe me, the only regret I have is that I can't kill you again. I hate you, Sonia! I'm not scared of you or Rafael any more. God made a mistake when he created your funky ass!"

I turned around to make sure no one was looking in my direction, and than I pulled my pants down and peed on top of Sonia and Rafael's graves. Then I spit on top of the cross that bore their name. It felt good to be able to keep a promise I had made to myself.

They say it takes a long time to heal from a tragic crime such as rape. Bullshit! The grim reality of my 14th birthday lived with me every day. There was nothing anyone could say to me to make me understand it. I opted not to talk about it because people always wanted to hand me the usual clichés, which only made me want to push their wigs back. *Don't tell me you understand! Don't tell me I should have sought help! Don't tell me I should have forgiven my parents! None of that shit mattered or was gonna give me back my virginity, or give me back my baby. If that was the case, then why didn't you let your father rape you? Better yet, why didn't you rape or sell your daughter*

*out for crack and see if she was going to forgive you. Idiots!*
*Y'all don't know my life, nor have y'all ever experienced what*
*I've gone through in life, so save the bullshit for someone else!*

When I arrived at Inez's house, she had lit candles all
around her cozy little living room, and placed gigantic soft
pillows in the middle of the floor. Hormones in the room were
raging, and Inez laid her "J-Lo-before-Mark-Anthony-pumped-
two-babies-in-her-physique" naked ass on top of the pillows,
legs wide open and wearing a bright smile. I gave her a seductive
stare as I watched her lick her fingers. "Wow!"

"The kitten is clean for you, boo!"

A feminine thrill shivered through my body just by staring
at Inez's fat and juicy coochie. I caressed her body with gentle
kisses. I eased between her thighs, giving her hot pussy a slow,
gentle brush with my tongue. She pressed her trembling legs
together in an effort to keep my tongue in her magic box, but I
pulled away.

"Don't stop! Please eat me out!" she begged, wanting and
needing more. Instead, I pushed her legs back to her shoulders
until her pussy popped up like a flat screen TV. I strapped on a
double headed dildo, inserted nine and a half inches deep into
my pussy, then I ran up in her in slow motion with the other
half. When our pussies were lip to lip, I ran my tongue across
her sweet lips. A groan of lust rose from her throat, and her lips
twitched. "Harder!" she moaned.

"Who's this good pussy belong to?" I asked her, bringing

her to her fourth orgasm.

"Oh my... oh my God! I'm cummin'! This is your pussy, boo!"

We both came at the same time. Lying beside Inez, breathless, I realized that no man could ever make a woman feel the pleasure another woman could. Inez was receiving sexual pleasure unlike anything she had ever had in her life. My heart kept pounding. I was still leaking from my pussy. There was nothing in the world that felt as good as cummin'... nothing like it.

"Ma, you're the best piece of ass I ever had!" Inez said to me while staring into my eyes.

"Likewise, baby."

"Just so you know, we're supposed to go see the Judge tomorrow afternoon. I'm curious Ma. Why are you so interested in him?"

I knew it was coming; typical woman pillow talk after some good-ass sex. Women always wanted to talk. "Inez, there are a lot of things I'd rather not involve you in. The less you know, the better off you are. That way if anything ever happens, you can't be involved."

"Are you serious, Ma? I mean for real, think about it. I'm already involved." Inez gave me the *"Bitch, please!"* look.

"Listen, I'll tell you what. If I tell you, I don't want you to ask me anymore questions on the subject, okay?"

"I promise, I won't."

"I'm interested in the Judge because he was the one responsible for me going to prison for twenty-one years. I'm not new to the city; I was born and raised here. When I was 14 going on 15, I gave birth to a baby girl, which was put up for adoption by my mother. I'm thinking, maybe the Judge can help me in finding my daughter." I left out a lot of the details on purpose. I gave Inez enough information to get her off my back.

When I was done, she looked at me and smiled. "I'm sure we can force the Judge to help you. As I said, he's into some real kinky shit. If we get him on tape, he would have to do whatever we ask him to do. Let me handle this, Ma. I got your back." Inez licked my pussy until I passed out from the powerful orgasm that had my world spinning in circles.

When I awoke the next morning, Inez and I jumped into the shower. Not even ten minutes after we were in the shower, we heard the doorbell ring. Inez got out of the shower and wrapped a towel around her naked body. Before she opened the door, she returned to the shower.

"Who's was that?" I asked as I got out of the shower and headed towards the bedroom.

"Some trick I used to fuck with back in the day. I don't know what the fuck she wants. I'ma just see what she's doing here."

"Let her know that you are accounted for."

"I will, baby."

"I'll be in the room if you need me to step to this bitch."

When Inez opened the door, a dark skinned Cuban chick walked in as if she lived there, speaking loudly. "Damn, baby! Why haven't you called me? I thought we were cool. Talk to me!"

The chick's voice was annoying as hell. I was tempted to walk into the living room, but I wanted to see how Inez was gonna handle her business.

"I told you already, I'm in a serious relationship now. We still cool, though."

"Cool! Nah, baby! Just last month when I was paying your bills we were partners, lovers, and now we just cool? You got to be out your mind! What, now you're back on the strictly-dickly shit?"

"You're talking from the side of your neck. So you either lower your tone of voice in my house, or you can leave my crib. But like I said, we'll still be cool if you want."

I could tell Inez was serious about keeping me around. Baby girl had a slew of dyke bitches paying her bills and keeping her laced up, but, she was only committed to one fly bitch, and that was me.

"Being cool entitles me to what?"

"Listen here, Brenda. I don't owe you shit, and you don't owe me nothing. You paid my bills because you wanted to. Being cool means just that; friends only."

"Before I bounce, do I get to meet your new man?" Brenda asked as she looked towards the bedroom.

"Sure! You want to meet my new man, no problem. Baby, why don't you come out her and meet my friend?" Inez shouted with a devilish smile.

I walked out of the bedroom wearing a pair of Christian

Louboutin shoes, some Frankie B. jeans and a Versace T-shirt that accented my hard nipples. For a split second the bitch looked like she'd just seen a ghost. Her face appeared familiar, but I couldn't remember where I knew her from. Then it dawned on me. *This was the bitch from the hospital!*

"What up, baby?" I asked, as I wrapped my hands around Inez's small waist and unloosened the towel she had around her body.

"Sweet Lips, this is Brenda. Brenda, this is Sweet Lips," Inez said while looking Brenda directly in her eyes.

"Haven't--"

"No, I don't think we've ever met. However, Inez is my woman, and I'd appreciate it if you'd respect that. I would love to get to know you a little better, but Inez and I have an important meeting we must attend, so thank you for stopping by." This ugly ass bitch stared at me as if I was saying some disrespectful shit to her. *I wish you would act crazy so I can beat some cuteness into your ass!*

As soon as she was out the door, I turned around and asked Inez, "What in the world are you doing with that butter-face, ugly bitch? Her paper's got to be long!" I shook my head in disbelief. Damn! This bitch looked like an ape! The only thing she had going for her was her body.

"She's just a trick who pays the bills," Inez responded as she slid her fat ass into an Ann Taylor skirt, a Gucci Tee, some Gucci stilettos. Then she slid on a pair of dark Gucci shades. She looked stunning; very ghetto fabulous.

We entered the Judge's chambers at the Criminal Justice Center in Philadelphia as if we were two high-ranking attorneys getting ready to crack open the case of the century. Judge Larry McCall had other ideas besides lunch on his mind, as evidenced by the fact that the entire carpet was covered with a plastic sheet.

"Good afternoon, ladies!" Judge McCall said as he got up from his desk and shut the door to his chambers and locking it from the inside. "Y'all looking hot!" he told Inez. In truth, the only thought on his mind was getting a golden shower.

Inez and I smiled at him. "Thank you, Your Honor!" Inez responded.

"How many times have I asked you to call me Larry?"

"About a thousand times," Inez said.

"I'm not up for lunch. I have to be in court in about an hour. How about if we stay here and just do the regular?"

"We could do that, Your Honor. However, we're gonna need your help on a few things. You see, my friend here, Sweet Lips, is trying to locate her daughter who was put up for adoption twenty-one years ago. Every agency she's been to has been giving her the normal bureaucracy bullshit. Can you help in this noble deed, Your Honor?" Inez unzipped his black robe, and I'll be damned! The good old judge was butt ass naked!

"I'll have my clerk look into it," he responded, touching himself.

"I know you will help, daddy." Inez winked at me.

The judge took his black robe off and lay his nasty, wrinkled ass on top of the plastic sheet. Inez lifted her skirt to her waist and squatted over his face. The judge closed his eyes and opened his mouth. I took my cell phone out of my bag, and like a professional photographer started snapping pictures of Inez pissing in the judge's mouth. When she was done, the judge looked at me and asked, "Will you join us?"

*Damned if I do and damned if I don't!* I unzipped my jeans and took Inez's place over his face. Right then, another idea crossed my mind. As I rubbed my pussy over the judge's mouth. I forced myself to shit in his face.

When he felt my shit dropping on this face, he yelled, "My God! I'm cumming!"

I smiled as I grabbed the hem of his black robe and wiped myself clean. The smell of shit made my stomach bubble.

"You nasty little girl! I like you!" The judge was all smiles as he got up from the floor and balled up the plastic for an easy cleanup. Then he washed his face and chest in the bathroom of his chambers. When he was robed again, he gave Inez an envelope and then looked at me. "I want to see you again. My clerk will facilitate you in your quest to locate your daughter. Make sure to arrange a meeting with him. I'm sorry about lunch, but I have to go," he said as he slid out of the side door which led to his courtroom.

I felt somewhat relieved knowing I wiped my ass with a symbol of justice; the judge's black robe. "Damn, baby girl! That's a freaky white man!" I whispered to Inez as we headed out of the Criminal Justice Center with a promise and seventy five hundred dollars in cold cash.

"This is one of the fringe benefits we get when we are willing and able to fulfill these powerful, freak ass white men's fantasies."

"Did you get the shot of me shitting on his face?"

"You know I did! That's the money shot, Ma!"

After we got back to Inez's place, I went in the bathroom and washed my ass, then I grabbed the list of agencies that Julio gave me and headed back out.

# CHAPTER 15
## "Secret Lovers"

By the end of the evening, I had managed to visit the agency responsible for the adoption of the four babies on my list. For the most part, each agency gave me the same bureaucracy bullshit: *"We're sorry. We are not allowed to reveal any information concerning adoptions."* Cutting through the red tape was proving to be harder than I had thought.

My call for help was answered sooner than I dared to hope. Apparently, a nice looking young counselor at the last agency I visited observed my sad expression and offered his services. I resisted his attempt at being a Good Samaritan, giving him the *"Nigga, please!"* look, but he made a gallant effort to make me smile.

Contemplating my next move I said, "I don't have time for any bullshit!" I put my hand around my midsection and stared into his eyes.

"I've always admired a fine woman with such an extensive vocabulary."

*I know this nigga ain't trying to clown me!* "Nigga, fuck you! You tight ass niggas always want to act like you're better than everybody else. Get the fuck out of my way!"

"What's wrong?"

"What's wrong is that your ass is about to get slapped for invading my space!" I said, putting my fingers up on his face.

"Relax!" he said. His voice was soft and hesitant, but when you are the head nigga in charge, you don't have to get hyped about things.

"Listen, this ain't the time for friendly talk. I'm looking for help in locating my daughter and I--"

"Follow me into my office. Let's see what we can do for you."

I followed him down a long corridor into an office with a sign on the door that read, "Supervisor".

"By the way, my name is William Raymosa. I'm the Supervisor."

"What a crazy way to meet. My name is Mita Cruz, and I'm searching for my daughter," I said while staring at him.

"If you don't mind me asking you, Ms. Cruz, how old are you? Because you look fairly young to be searching for a daughter."

"Mr. Raymosa, a woman never tells her age. Nevertheless, I'm 32 years old. I had my daughter when I was fourteen years old. So, how can you help me? Or are you just wasting my time?"

"I could help you. But by now I'm sure you are familiar with the procedures, right?"

"Yes, I'm familiar with them."

"So you do understand that any help I give you never came from me," he said with a concerned smile.

"Look, I understand you're not supposed to give me any

information concerning adoption, so whatever help you give me will be kept a secret."

"So that means we got an understanding, right?"

"Yes, we do. What do I have to do for this help?"

"Nothing. I know how biased the system can be. I sympathize with you."

*This nigga is up to no good, offering me help for nothing. I know he don't think I'm that slow.* William, in the seat across from me, was watching me with a bewildered smile. "Are you this helpful to everyone?" I asked.

He nodded vigorously. "What's wrong with helping someone in need?"

"Nothing."

Never once did he crack for pussy, and he treated me like a human being instead of a piece of ass. For a minute I was beginning to think that he was gay or something. He pulled all the strings he could to get me to step closer to finding my daughter. By the end of the day, he had managed to pull the files of all four babies born on September 13, 1990, in Temple Hospital. Everything in the foster care system was done by codes, so he couldn't come up with the names. But he did manage to locate the addresses to where those four babies were placed after leaving the hospital. He also discovered that in most cases, babies put up for adoption were not identified by race or gender, but by a code assigned to each case file.

"It's a shame, isn't it?" I said.

"Very sad," William said. "But every code is meant to be

broken. Most babies put up for adoption get lost in the system. If they're lucky, they end up with a halfway decent family. I say halfway, because most of the time, most foster care children end up in low income homes, with families who use the foster care system as a hustle for the fat monthly checks they receive. Statistics show that 70% of the children in foster care are most likely to offend as adults."

"What are the chances of me finding my daughter after all these years?"

"I will say very slim. Don't get your hopes up," he said with a shrewd glance at me.

"I'm not a sensible woman."

"Good, because locating foster and adopted children can become painful. Sometimes the children are content with how their lives are going and don't care much about their biological parents. In many cases the children are young adults and don't even know they are adopted. So there are ups and down to this."

William's lecture did nothing to soothe my restlessness. My thoughts jumped from Inez to finding my daughter, and back to William again. I needed a promising lead, and William had given it to me. But his remarks had also given me something else to think about. *What if my daughter didn't want to meet me? What if she was happy with her current life? What if she was married?* I'm not sure if I could handle her rejection well. For the first time in a long time, fear gripped me.

"Are you alright?" William asked with a concerned smile.

"I'm alright."

"It's not an easy process. You must be strong. Tomorrow, if you have the time, I will help you set up a My Space account, and a Face Book and Twitter account. We must use all the technology available to us to get the message out."

When I reached Inez's crib, I thought the place was empty, until I heard the voices of two females. I recognized one, Inez's. The other had me intrigued. The hinges of Inez's door had been oiled, so they didn't hear me entering the apartment. The bedroom door was ajar, and the conversation was crystal clear. At first, I thought Inez had another bitch in bed. I didn't want to jump the gun without being sure, so I just stood by the bedroom door, listening to their conversation.

"...Does she know who you really are?" the unidentified voice asked Inez.

"No. Nobody knows. I've been undercover for the last seven months, and I'm real close to building my case against the judge and all his flunkies."

*Undercover! Hell nah! This bitch can't be the police. Hell nah! I must be hearing shit. I can't believe I been sexing the fucking police, an CIA agent at that! Hell nah!* I thought to myself as I listen to Inez plea her case to the unidentified woman.

"Time is running out. The brass up top is only giving us two more months. I feel we have enough evidence to bring these bastards down now. If you fuck this case up, your career is over. You will be on shit duty."

"I'm playing my part, but I need more time. I don't want these assholes to plead. I want a solid case."

"Yeah, you're playing your part, by fucking a convicted murderer. I done my homework on that little, pretty bitch you been running around with. As your supervisor, I must be honest with you. I'm giving you leeway to build your case and to live your life undercover as you see fit to do. My only concern is your little girlfriend. After reviewing her files, I must say she has quite a background; two counts of involuntary manslaughter. If my superiors get wind of this, both of our asses will be done. You do know that what you are engaging in is unethical?"

"Save the textbook bullshit for the Academy. I'm the one who's putting my life in danger. The government knew about my sexual preferences when they hired me."

I was getting upset that this bitch was even bringing my personal life up in this conversation.

"Yes, indeed we knew your sexual preference. The problem is that you're involving your girlfriend in this case. That can become a conflict of interest."

"I told you already, her being involved is a coincidence. McCall was the judge who sent her to prison. I didn't know that. She's on a mission to find her daughter. Whatever she does to bring this pervert down can only reinforce my case."

*This bitch thinks she's going to use me! Fuck her CIA, cop ass. I'ma use her to find my daughter then I'm out. I'm not about to be wifey to no police.* I told myself, enjoying the conversation.

"You're playing with fire."

"I'm a grown ass woman."

"You are also an CIA Agent who took an oath to protect and serve."

"Am I not living up to my oath?"

"Yes, you are, but like I said, you're playing with fire."

"My personal love life has nothing to do with my job. I'm entitled to love whoever I want, right?"

"She's a convicted felon with a violent past!"

"Don't we all have some dirt in our closet? Right now you are sounding like a jealous bitch. Let me see. When we hooked up, wasn't that unethical? But no, when you do it, it's cool, right? What would the brass up top say if they found out that their most trusted supervisor in the department was sleeping with a rookie agent, and that I was assigned to this case, not because of my street smarts, but because I was sleeping with you?"

*I knew these two whores were lovers. What the fuck have I gotten myself into?* I thought to myself.

"What we had was just a one night thing, and no, I'm not jealous. I'm just concerned about the whole situation. You have my blessing and support on this."

"Like I stated, Agent Yolanda Rivas! My personal life is my business, and I fuck whoever I want to fuck, whenever I want to. I knew your ass would bring this up. Trust me, if you even think about leaking any information about me on this, I promise you one thing, you won't lick another pussy in your life, because we both be searching for new jobs. Act funny if you want to!" Inez said as she slid two fingers into her wet pussy and slid them under Agent Rivas nose, then added, "But if you act like you got some sense, maybe I'll let you lick this hot ass pussy again. Now, get the fuck out my apartment! I'm waiting on my convicted felon girl," she said with a smirk.

"It's like that huh!"

"Yeah bitch, it's like that. As I said, act crazy if you want to."

Before Agent Yolanda Rivas was able to walk out of the room, I managed to hurry back out to the living room. When she saw me, her face turned all different colors. She rolled her eyes and stared at me with hate and lust at the same time. *"Yeah bitch, I'm down with your game!"* I licked my lips and smiled, because she knew that I knew that Inez's cover was blown. My only worry was, who really was Inez? If she was undercover, that meant that she's probably using a fake name. I needed answers.

"Inez! You have company!" Agent Rivas yelled as she walked out of the door.

Inez came out the room in her underwear looking all sexy as if nothing had transpired.

"Damn baby! When did you get here?"

"I've been here for a while. I just didn't want to interrupt your conversation with your supervisor, lover, whoever the fuck that ugly bitch was," I said with a serious face, looking Inez straight in her eyes.

"Wait a minute, baby. I can explain."

"Explain what! That your ass is the police? That your ass been playing me, trying to use me to bring down the judge?

Bitch, I may be a convicted felon, but I don't have stupid written on my face!"

Inez just looked as if she wasn't understanding me. "Yeah, I'm a CIA agent, but so what! I never judged you or even came at you on some cop shit. I don't bring my job home with me. I don't mix my personal life with my job."

"You still ain't saying shit! I feel like you played me into a fake relationship. I don't fuckin' even know your real name. As far as I'm concerned, you are a phony bitch. Plus, I don't fuck with the police. I hate the police!"

"Ma, it is what it is. I never lied to you. Yeah, I may have left out some information, but I never lied to you. My real name is Evita Inez Rivera, and as you already know, I'm an CIA agent. Now, we could ride with this shit out together, or you could step right now. However, my little friend who just left seems to have a problem with us fucking around, and with her position, she could create a lot of problems for both of us."

*I lied abut my name being Evita Inez Rivera, because even though she already knows I'm an CIA agent, she still didn't know the full story. Plus, I've been trained to act my way out of certain situations.*

"Was you fucking her?" I asked Inez Evita, whatever the fuck her name was.

"Yeah. We messed around one time."

"One time only? By the way she was coming at your neck; it appeared like she was still claiming you."

"Ma, that bitch is crazy. She don't have a life outside of

the CIA. She's irrelevant. What matters to me is you. So, are you going to ride with me or not?"

*"Damn! This little bitch is serious about me. I might as well play her game and see what I can gain from it After all, I got nothing to lose.* Baby girl, there are rules to this shit we call a relationship. If we're going to ride together, then you can't keep me in the dark about your job or identity. You've got to be honest with me, feel me?"

"I feel you, but you already know my true identity. From now on, life will be beautiful for you. I promise Ma." Inez said, dropping to her knees in from of me.

Her thong was under her ass. She lifted her fat ass and tossed her thong at me. It caught on the end of my nose. I stopped them from falling and inhaled. I can't front, the smell of her pussy had me dripping like a water fountain.

"So are we going to ride together, Ma?"

"Baby girl, just suck my clit the way you know how. I got your back," I said.

"Wow, what a dream cum true!" Inez said, twirling and whirling her tongue until we both were breathless.

# CHAPTER 16
### "It's Almost Over"

Special Agent Jasmine Rodriguez had been searching for her biological mother since the age of thirteen. Every week faithfully she'd search the Internet, logging on to dozens of sites. Her My Space page, under the pseudonym *"Lost Daughter Looking For Mother"* generated hundreds of hits daily from across the country, but none of them had led anywhere. Today, however, she stared at her laptop computer screen. One new My Space page had caught her attention. She clicked the little icon, and the whole page came up:

> *If you were born on September 13, 1990, In Temple University Hospital, Philadelphia, PA, and if you were adopted and are interested in reconnecting with your biological mother, leave a message.*

Could this be her? This can't be a coincidence. Same birthplace, same birth date: mother looking for her daughter. A creeping feeling in the pit of her stomach caused her to groan. She typed her message:

> *I read your My Space page, and I'm*

*wondering if we could be related. My
name is Jasmine Rodriguez, and I fit the
description you gave in your My Space
page. I see we're in the same city, so it
wouldn't be a problem for me to arrange
a meeting with you. Even if nothing comes
out of this meeting, at least we would be
clear of all doubts. So, if by the time you
receive this message you haven't located
your daughter, maybe we should meet
and compare family backgrounds. Peace.*

She re-read the message and then hit the return button.

By society's standards, Special Agent Jasmine Rodriguez had beaten the odds. She had taken full advantage of the opportunities the foster care and adoption system had to offer, such as free public college tuition, graduating summa cum laude with a degree in law enforcement. She had become the youngest federal agent in the city of Philadelphia. She had also managed to avoid all the stereotypical bullshit that adopted and foster children are branded with, such as teen pregnancy, unemployment and imprisonment. From the outside, she was looked on as the poster child for the adoption system, but behind closed doors, she was fighting truckloads of demons; she was damaged goods, and her soul was lost.

She leaned back on her bed. Tears flowed down her cheeks, and for the first time in her life, she felt loved. Although her relationship with Sweet Lips had its up and downs, for the most part, it was all good She actually saw herself being around Sweet Lips for a long time.

Special Agent Jasmine Rodriguez was caught up in the rapture when her cell phone went off went off. It signaled an emergency call. For a second she thought about not answering it because she was waiting on a call from her connection at the Human Services Department, but she backpedaled on her thoughts.

"It's going down next week, Friday. The brass up top wants this case wrapped up now, so the plan has changed."

"What? How could this be? When?"

"They run the show, and we must follow their game plan. It is what it is, so make sure you have all your reports ready for me."

"Why so soon?"

"I just left a conference with U.S. Attorney Charles Krinsky, and the faggot is ambitious and banking his career on this case, so we've got to wrap it up next week."

"I can't believe this! After all the work I've done for the Department, now they want to fuck me on this case! I'm beginning to feel like you had something to do with this, but I'm not one to sweat the small shit, and you have proven to me how small your jealous ass is. You'd better hope this shit doesn't come back and bite you in the ass, and you better not even think about crossing me, because if you do, I swear to you, I will bring you down!"

"Listen here, little girl. Your threats don't move me. And just for the record, I had nothing to do with this call. But you can think whatever you want. At the end of the day, I'm your supervisor, and that means you jump when I tell you to jump. So be prepared. As a matter of fact, you are on call twenty four hours a day starting today, and that's an order!"

"No problem! You're the boss!"

"I'm glad you recognize that I'm the head bitch in charge!"

As soon as she got off the phone, Special Agent Jasmine Rodriguez made the phone call that would set her plan in motion.

"Hello?"

"Listen, Ma. My supervisor is on some shady shit. Meet me at my place at 5:30 p.m. We must move out on our plans."

*If this bitch thinks she's gonna play me, she got something else coming her way. I'ma show her she ain't as slick as she thinks she is.*

# CHAPTER 17
### "Freak in the Bed"

By the time I arrived at Inez's house, she was already there waiting for me in her thong. My lips instantly watered. No matter how much dick William was laying on me, I still had an appetite for her pussy. Inez had the kind of pussy that just kept my tongue on fire. I could lick her pussy all day and wouldn't get tired. No words needed to be spoken. I walked behind her, bent her over the windowsill, spread her delicious ass cheeks and tossed her salad, sliding three fingers inside her asshole.

"Tongue fuck me, *Mami!* Smack me hard!" Inez was weak in the knees. She struggled to keep her balance.

I reached into my jeans pocked and pulled out an ecstasy pill that I had taken from Solo, and placed it on the tip off my tongue, and then I shoved it up Inez's asshole. "I miss this pussy, baby. Make those pussy lips clap for me."

Inez was shaking uncontrollably. After twenty minutes of tongue fucking her, the ecstasy pill started taking effect. She started bouncing her ass up and down on my face as if she was a video whore. She needed more of my magic tongue. "Let's go to the bedroom, baby," I said to her. Once in the bedroom, I made her lay on her stomach. Then I popped open a bottle of champagne and poured it down the crack of her ass. Once the bottle was empty, I inserted the bottleneck into her asshole an inch at a time, expanding it to the size of a softball.

"Damn, baby, that feels good! I'm cumming! Give it to me harder, *Mami!* I'm cumming!"

I started to stroke the bottle feverishly in and out of her ass, watching the neck disappear. The smell of her booty was driving me crazy. She gave loud groan. The ecstasy pill had her humping her fat ass even harder.

"Oh, my God, I'm cumming!"

I played with her clit.

"*Si! Si! Si! Si! Si!* Punish me, Ma!"

Inez came so hard that she passed out. When I pulled the bottle out of her ass, it took a while to tighten back up to its normal size.

After Inez regained her senses, we took a shower together. The warm water against my body made me ready to do some more freak shit to my young prized possession.

"That was the best orgasm, I ever had. Thank you!"

"Anything for you, baby. Let's do it again tonight," I whispered into her ear while rubbing her nipples.

"So, tell me, baby. Do you think your supervisor is stupid enough to expose our relationship to the media?" I asked her while we lay in bed.

"If she does, it will be my word against hers, and at most they'll likely believe her because she is a high ranking official of the department. But I've got a surprise for her. I've got some dirt on her that would make her think twice about crossing me.

Remember, I have the same CIA training that she does. Right now, we must set our plan in motion for early Monday morning. The Feds are going to be handing down indictments on the judge, Solo, and everyone involved in the kiddy porn ring." Inez gave me the insolent look that could be found on a cop who's on a mission.

I listened to Inez without worrying about anything, because from being around her, I knew she didn't give a proverbial rat's ass about her supervisor.

"If she thinks she's suddenly gonna be Federal Agent of the Year or something, she's wrong. It's way too late for that. I can't believe her! I'm looking forward to helping you put your plans in motion. I got your back, baby."

I shrieked with rage. With so much at stake, Inez's supervisor may fuck around and become AWOL.

# CHAPTER 18

## "This Is How We Do It"

"Judge, it's always an honor to see you," I said after giving him a hug. Inez and I noticed the plastic on the floor and instantly smiled. The fucking pervert thought we were there to shit in his mouth.

"My two favorite girls! I must be dying and going to heaven tonight."

*Heaven! I don't think so. You're going to booty land where real niggas with big dicks are gonna be honored to run their dicks up in your ass, raw.*

"I'm glad you feel blessed, because we got something important do discuss," Inez winked at the Judge as she gave him a good view of her pussy. Her skirt was rolled up to her waistline.

"Sweeties, whatever I could do for you ladies, I'm here!" the Judge said, drooling all over himself.

"As a matter of act, there is something you can do for us. We want to watch some of those kiddy porn movies you've been acting in. Better yet, we want to watch this one here!" Inez stared the judge straight in the eyes as she pulled out a DVD from the inside of her bag.

The Judge smiled as he wondered why we were making such a request. Still, it was a turn-on for him. "I didn't know y'all were intrigued by such acts, but now that I do, we definitely can watch a few." He slid the DVD inside the DVD player. When the screen lit up, he literally pissed in his pants. His jaw almost dropped to the floor, and his false teeth fell out of his mouth. Up on the screen, he was doing his thing with two little girls who appeared to be no more than eleven or twelve years old.

"Oh, don't panic now, Your Honor. There's more," I said with a smile.

The screen showed the Judge lying on top of a sheet of plastic on the floor in his chambers while a naked girl squatted over him and shit on his face. I was impressed with how good of a job Inez did at editing the film to conceal our identities.

"You see, Judge, all this could disappear in a matter seconds if you let us in on the scene." Inez got up from her chair and stood in front of him.

"Y'all sheisty bitches! Nobody will believe you! Do you know who I am?"

Inez and I both laughed at his toughness.

"Ma, can you imagine how the ratings on that bitch, Nancy Grace's show are going to be once she gets a hold of this DVD and airs it for the world to see?" Inez twisted her lips up, blowing a kiss to the Judge.

"You two bitches are trying to blackmail me?"

"No, Your Honor, that's against the law. Actually, we're trying to save you from jail. We just want a piece of the pie. Ain't that the American way?"

"That DVD proves nothing!"

"Your Honor, I think you should watch the whole tape. Trust me, you will enjoy it." Inez hit the play button on the remote control. The next scene was of the Judge getting fucked in the ass by a dark, skinny man who appeared to have a long dick. Freak ass Solo was putting a dent in the judge's asshole. The tape ended with the Judge and a man I knew all too well exchanging money and boxes of DVDs.

"So, are we convincing you now, Your Honor? Because if we're not, I wouldn't want to waste any more of your valuable time."

I could feel the Judge struggling for breath under Inez's pressure, and I was enjoying it. I was determined to see him sacrifice his comfort for the greater good. I mean, I was a lesbian, so by no means was I a crusader for morality. My sexual lifestyle dictated otherwise. But as a victim of child abuse, it was my mission to administer my own brand of justice to these assholes out here who got off by fucking little girls and boys.

"You two bitches will pay for this!"

"Your Honor, you are the one who's going to be paying for this! Plus, your threats are falling on deaf ears. For the record, my woman here already paid with twenty-one years of her life in prison. Remember her? Look at her. Doesn't she look familiar? Your nasty ass was the one who put her there. So now it's your time to pay. We want two million dollars in cash by tomorrow morning, and I don't want to hear the bullshit that you don't have that kind of money, because I've been watching you, and I do know that you have a separate bank account from your wife. I also know that your kiddy porn business generates eighty thousand dollars a month. So just have our money ready tomorrow, because if you don't, you can consider yourself done. Your Honor, just out of curiosity, where are you planning to take your wife for your 30th anniversary on Friday?"

"Fuck you, you little criminal! God doesn't like ugly!"

"So he must hate you, because you are one ugly mothafucka! Have my money by tomorrow morning, ten O'clock. Have a nice day, Your Honor!"

Inez and I exited the judge's chambers feeling vindicated.

At the National Bank, Solo sat behind his desk in a lavish office, while his assistant, a young-butt boy, sucked his dick, bringing him to tears. Solo was so far gone that he didn't even hear us entering his office.

*This one was going to be easy.*

"Oh, shit!" he yelled when he opened his watery eyes and saw Inez and I standing in front of his desk.

"Don't worry. Do your thing," I said as I watched the young-butt boy swallow Solo's dick completely, wrapping his long tongue around it.

*Damn! This punk got some skills!* Was the only thing I could think of. There was no shame in Solo's game. He didn't discriminate. He got his freak on whichever way it came. He caught and pitched. When the butt-boy was done, he got up and immediately locked lips with Solo, transferring all the cum he had just sucked out of his nuts into Solo's mouth. Solo swallowed proudly.

"Listen Solo, we don't have much time, but I think you will be interested in this," Inez said as she slid the DVD into the DVD player.

Solo stared in disbelief as he saw himself getting his back blown out by the mayor's brother in the mayor's office. "You mothafuckas!" he whispered.

"If I was you, I'd be quiet. Right now you're in no position to be running your mouth," Inez said with a serious expression as she fast forwarded the DVD until she reached the scene where Solo had his tongue deep in the Judge's ass, licking his own cum.

"Ugh! That's nasty!" I whispered as Inez kept staring at Solo.

"So what? I'm tri-sexual. This is 2009. Most men in our society are gay. This is bogus shit. What does it prove?"

"Oh, I got some more. Watch this." Inez fast forwarded the DVD again, this time stopping it at a scene where Solo was sodomizing a young boy who couldn't have been older than fourteen. "You see this? In Pennsylvania this is called 'rape'. That young boy is fourteen years old."

"No way! He told me he was twenty! It was consensual sex between two adults.

"Are you willing to take that chance in a courtroom?"

Solo was at a loss for words. He couldn't afford to have this DVD splashed all over the city. He spoke nonchalantly.

"What's the twist to all this?"

"I thought you would never ask. We want two million dollars in cash by tomorrow morning. I don't even want to hear the bullshit, 'Where am I going to get that kind of money from?' I did my homework on your ass. Your kiddy porn ring generates eighty grand or more a month, and you've been running this shit now for six years, so I know two-mil is change in your pockets. If you play stupid, this DVD will be on You Tube, CNN, Fox 29, Nancy Grace, and every news station in the Tri-state. Don't bitch up now, punk boy! You got the money. Have my shit by tomorrow at nine a.m.," Inez said in a bitter, unsympathetic tone.

Now the waiting began. I wasn't worried, because Inez was on some real cop shit, and she had these two freak mothafuckas' backs against the wall.

# CHAPTER 19

### "I Need Love"

I walked into Kinkos with my shoes clacking against the floor, feeling excited about becoming a millionaire within the next twenty-four hours on account of two perverts. When I reached the front of the line, the clerk was a young Chinese chick. She escorted me to the computer room and explained to me the per-minute pricing. *Bitch, I been using this system for over a month now!* I was about to tell her, but thought better of it. I handed her a twenty-dollar bill and signed on to the Web. I typed in my Web handle, Yourmother.Myspace.com. The screen rolled into view, and at the top it read:

*You have one email in your box.*

My heart began to pump fast and tears began to roll down my face. I clicked on the New Mail icon and wiped my tears away. The email message appeared.

*I read your My Space page, and I'm wondering if we could be related. My name is Jasmine Rodriguez, and I fit the description you gave in your My Space page. I see we're in the same city, so it wouldn't be a problem for me to arrange a meeting with you. Even if nothing comes out of this meeting, at lest we would be clear of all doubts. So,*

*if by the time you receive this message you haven't*
*located your daughter, maybe we should meet and*
*compare family backgrounds. Peace.*

I was trying to gather up any internal strength, when I saw
the Chinese clerk staring at me as if I was going to steal the
damn computer. My hands shook as I began to type a message:

*Jasmine, I would very much like to meet*
*with you. How about Friday at 11:00 a.m. at Isla*
*Verde Restaurant? Lunch is on me. I'll be wearing*
*Plick jeans and white T-shirt.*

I pressed the return button. For a long while, I sat in front
of the screen just re-reading Jasmine's message. After my half-
hour was up, I closed my page and treated myself to a shopping
spree down on Market Street.

Special Agent Jasmine Rodriguez sat behind her desk at
the Federal Building, viewing her personal emails. She kept her
finger on the delete button, deleting all the junk email, Spam,
and bulk mail. She narrowed her eyes and hit the right scroll
button. She read the last email over and over again. *Damn! Out*
*of all the days of the week, she wants to meet on Friday at Isla*
*Verde. What a coincidence!*

Friday's schedule was already set aside for the raid, but
one way or another, she was going to meet with the author of
the email. How, she had no idea. For the first time in her life
she was scared. As bad as she wanted to meet her real mother,
emotionally she wasn't sure if she was prepared.

She got up from her desk and went into the bathroom, splashed cold water on her face and then checked herself out in the mirror. Tears filled her eyes and her heart crumbled and soared all at once. *I must find my real mother. I need a family.* Nobody understood what it felt like to be an adopted child with no family. It was like a parasite feeding off the misery of the innocents.

People say that tragedy was good for the soul. Bullshit! The worst tragedy a living person could suffer was not knowing where they came from. Some might argue that her accomplishments served as an example for others. In part, that was true. But it didn't matter what kind of car she drove, what degrees she had, or what job she worked in. She was still a lost soul with a chip on her shoulder.

Strangely enough, she specialized in crushing men who thought they couldn't be touched. Her hate towards men came from not having a father figure in her life, and her love towards me came from her not having a mother in her life.

# CHAPTER 20
## "Bad News"

I knew the symptoms all too well. It was like my past all over again as I sat on the floor with my face in the toilet bowl, throwing up. There was no doubt in my mind, but to make sure, I decided to walk down to the pharmacy and purchase an over-the-counter test.

Once back in my studio apartment, I tore the box open, pulled out the small strip, by-passed the directions, sat on the toilet and forced myself to pee on the strip. After placing the strip back into the test kit, I waited a few minutes; then all my fears were answered... I was pregnant. There was no question on who the father was. I'd only been fucking one nigga raw-dog, and that was William.

"Dear God!" I muttered and tried to imagine the horror of raising a child on my own. I lay in my bed crying, trying to find a direction for my scattered thoughts. Finding out that I was pregnant had me feeling tired and achy.

I'd been seeing a nigga raw, not even knowing whether he had AIDS or not. What the fuck was I to expect? I couldn't have this baby. What would Inez think? How would she feel? This had to be a mistake. I got out of bed and grabbed the calendar from the wall and started counting the days. How could I be so careless? I thought about what this child would look like, and whether it was a girl or a boy.

I searched the Yellow Pages until I found the number to a gynecologist and made an appointment. Two hours later, I found myself butt-ass-naked, wrapped in a paper gown, and my knees spread wide on a table waiting for the doctor to make his diagnosis.

"Ms. Cruz, I'm guessing you are around six weeks pregnant," he announced with a grin, then added, "Is this your first child?"

It was exactly the wrong shit to ask me. My face flushed and my eyes glared angrily. "You know, doctor, I don't think it's any of your business!" I got my ass off the table and scrambled into my clothes. I wanted to get the fuck out of the office. I couldn't wait to tell Inez.

I panicked with my panties halfway up. *Tell Inez? And tell her I'd been fucking a nigga raw who I barely knew, and I was pregnant! Or I should I have just called William and said, "Hi, you're going to be a father!"*

I finished dressing with a bad taste in my mouth. My body trembled as the thought of being a mother invaded my mind. I couldn't bear the thought of bringing an innocent life into this fucked up world. I was afraid I would be just like my mother. Was I worthy of having a child?

*"You're nothing like your mother! Look at me, baby! If you aren't brave enough to trust yourself, then trust me to do it for you. Don't blame yourself for the mistakes your mother made.*

*Crucifying yourself with the past will only make you bitter. It will stress you out, and you've already endured a lot."* Those were the last words Mrs. Penny said to me on our last visit together.

Until her death, Sonia Cruz, my mother had been my only role model. What kind of mother could I be when the only one I ever knew was nothing but an abusive, unfit bitch? I didn't have anyone besides Mrs. Penny in my childhood teaching me how to become a woman. Everything I knew about surviving as a woman, I learned in prison.

As I walked into my apartment, I felt the nausea welling up in the pit of my stomach. I made it to the toilet just as my guts gust erupted. *I can't believe this shit is happening to me!* I vomited again. My face flushed with sudden anger as I looked at myself in the mirror. I slammed both of my palms down on top of the sink counter. *This baby's got to go! I'm not prepared to be a mother!*

# CHAPTER 21

### "Sweet Home"

Once Jasmine Rodriguez was settled inside Special Agent Yolanda Rivas' apartment, she snapped on a pair of latex gloves. Like most CIA agents, Yolanda Rivas had files of open cases neatly piled up on the kitchen table. A nice flat screen TV sat on an ordinary entertainment cabinet, but what looked like an expensive collection of DVDs dominated the wall opposite the living room's solitary couch.

Jasmine Rodriguez placed a DVD into the player and pressed play. Up on the TV screen, Agent Rivas could be seen getting her pussy pounded out of the frame. Jasmine smiled to herself, because Yolanda had secrets of her own. She took a quick tour of the apartment to make sure she was indeed alone. She was.

Special Agent Yolanda Rivas' bed was neat, but full of more surprises. The queen size bed had two poles on each side, with leather straps and handcuffs attached to them. Jasmine methodically checked under the mattress and removed a .45 she had kept there, and on the nightstand a box of extra large condoms sat neatly.

She made it back to the living room preparing for her mission. The duffel bags she had bought with her were loaded with all the tools a Federally trained assassin would need to accomplish a mission; handcuffs, stun gun, duct tape, and an unregistered gun with a silencer.

After two hours, Yolanda Rivas stepped into the elevator and headed up to her apartment. The Liberty Plaza apartments were home to the exclusive and privileged crowd in Philadelphia. The smell of sex mingled in the air, which was probably some white bitch giving a rich nigga some ass in the elevator. That seemed to be the norm amongst the privileged. Niggas still hadn't learned shit after the O.J. fiasco. However, Agent Rivas liked coming home at night after a hard day's work. The solitude of her apartment made her feel at peace.

Her mind started drifting back to the conversation she'd had three days ago with Special Agent Jasmine Rodriguez. She appeared to be upset about having to wrap her assignment up.

When she stuck the key in the door and walked in, she was struck with a sharp pain, powerful enough to bring her to her knees. The stun gun ran electricity straight to her kidneys. Special Agent Yolanda Rivas crumbled to the floor without a clue of what was taking place.

Immediately, Jasmine pulled out a pair of handcuffs and secured her prisoner. Then she duct taped her mouth shut, and dragged Rivas to her bedroom and tied her legs to the bed pole. Then she placed an ice pick under her rib cage, poking her until she reached the liver. Agent Rivas' eyes bulged. Jasmine chose an ice pick for this mission because she didn't want to make a mess. She wanted her target to bleed internally.

The pain was beyond anything Agent Rivas had ever imagined. Her fate was sealed, and she knew it.

"Ain't this how they train us at the Academy? Torture the prisoner from the start? Ain't this how they do it?" she asked Agent Rivas, poking her again in the liver and twisting the ice pick with passion.

Rivas' screams were cut short by the duct tape, and only shit and piss escaped her. Special Agent Rivas whimpered like a dying animal.

"Bitch, I want you to understand something! You may be the boss, but I'm the bitch who will decide if you live or die. I'm not gonna let you fuck my thing up all because you're on some jealous shit. Don't worry, at your funeral I will speak highly of you."

Special Agent Rivas' eyes were wide and uncomprehending. Her mind was too far gone.

Jasmine pressed the ice pick against her chest, and plunged into her, bursting her heart in two.

Agent Rivas' world fell silent.

The U.S. Attorney, Charles Krinsky didn't panic right away when Special Agent Yolanda Rivas didn't show up for her daily briefing. Agent Rivas often showed up late… very late… sometimes three or four hours late.

At 4:30 p.m., concern turned into fear. U.S. Attorney Charles Krinsky's call made Special Agent Jasmine Rodriguez come in her panties.

"No, I haven't heard from her since yesterday," Agent Rodriguez said groggily, pretending she was asleep.

The U.S. Attorney explained the situation. Jasmine, who was already dressed, promised to be at the CIA's downtown office in Philadelphia in twenty minutes. When she arrived at the CIA building, Charles Krinsky was waiting in front with four more agents.

Special Agent Rivas' apartment door was ajar. Charles pushed it open and yelled, "Yolanda!" No answer. He called her name again. Still no answer. The other five agents spread out through the apartment. The smell of death dominated when Charles entered the master bedroom. Something distinctly inhuman made the hair on the back of his neck stand up. Special Agent Rodriguez was coming out of the bathroom in time to hear the screams. "Noooooooo!"

Detective Scott Jones and Patrick McCullough of the Homicide Division arrived first on the scene, even before the uniforms. Patrick a greasy-haired Irishman who, in his spare time, wrote novels and taught math at Villanova University. He took the lead. He barked orders to the uniforms as they arrived. "Seal the fucking crime scene now, asshole!" he yelled to a young rookie who appeared to be lost and staring at the two lab technicians from the Crime Scene Unit. "Hey, asshole, isolate the witnesses!" Patrick said.

"But, sir, all the witnesses are CIA agents," the young rookie cop said, looking pale in the face.

"I don't give a rat's ass shit if Jesus is in here! I said isolate the witnesses, now!"

The rookie cop gathered the U.S. Attorney and the five CIA agents, and took their names. Normally, the U.S. Attorney would dress to impress, but the asshole had shit on himself when he found Special Agent Rivas' body.

"You okay?" Detective Jones asked, like he cared, putting a finger under his nose.

Charles Krinsky nodded.

Detective Scott Jones asked what brought them to the crime scene.

"After Special Agent Rivas failed to report to work, and after several attempts to reach her by phone, myself and five of my agents decided to come check on her, because it was unusual that she didn't report to work."

"Does the victim have any enemies in the department?" Detective Jones asked with an ugly, cynical smirk on his lips, which reflected both his total triumph and his total contempt. There was no secret that the Homicide Division shared a deep hatred towards the local CIA when it came to high profile cases, because the CIA agents in Philly walked around with their heads up their asses.

"Not to my knowledge."

"Well, from the looks of things, someone had a real hard-on for the victim," Detective Jones said as he looked directly into the eyes of U.S. Attorney Charles Krinsky. "You know the procedure. Every agent in here is a suspect until we can rule them out. You do know that PPD has jurisdiction over this case. I expect to see you and your agents at Homicide soon. The quicker we gather your statements, the faster will can begin the search for the killer or killers."

"Let's skip the bureaucratic bullshit! We can go to homicide now!" Charles Krinsky felt offended and disrespected that a fucking detective was treating him like a suspect in the death of one of his most trusted CIA agents.

"Sir, there is no need to get upset."

"Detective Jones, let me remind you of who I am. I'm the U.S. Attorney of Pennsylvania, and--"

"Sir, I know who you are. But let me remind you! Right now you and your agents are the only suspects and/or witnesses, and you are being treated as such. I'm sure you understand the law, right?"

The lab technician walked over to Detective Jones and said, "Sir, I think you'd better take a look at this." He pointed towards the DVD player in the living room.

After watching the video for a few seconds Jones said, "Gather all the evidence carefully and photograph everything." Then he turned to the U.S. Attorney Charles Krinsky and said, "I'm a narcissistic asshole, but I do my job well. I expect you and your agent to be at homicide in twenty minutes." He walked away, leaving the U.S. Attorney looking distraught.

# CHAPTER 22
## "My Way or The Highway"

Detective Patrick McCullough prided himself on his intelligence. With a Ph.D. in criminology and the keen ability to handle high profile cases with sensitivity and wit, he was a star among the ranks. He could've been Commissioner, but he loved working homicide so much that he requested not to be considered for promotion.

"What was that all about?" Patrick asked his partner.

"Nothing I can't handle. The dick-head Charles feels upset that I want to question him and his agents," Detective Scott Jones said, then turned his attention back to the lab technician. "This whole apartment should be considered a crime scene, not just the bedroom."

"Crime scene tape this whole apartment. Make sure nobody contaminates it more than what it is. And make sure the body is not removed until I examine it first. Can you handle that?" Detective McCullough asked the lab technician. He turned to his partner, Scott Jones. "Goddamn! Who the fuck does shit like this?"

"A mothafucker we have to catch. Whoever did this knows what he's doing. I'm willing to put my life on the line that this crime was not a random act. This was personal. When was the last time you saw a murder committed with an ice pick?"

Detective McCullough asked, eyebrows lifted, but otherwise expressionless.

Detective Jones studied his partner for a second. Once he finished observing him, he said, "We both know that every murder is different; the weapons, the degree and the level of brutality. This one here smells like a crime of passion. My guess--my belief--is that whoever did this must be suffering from some very traumatic shit."

"This is a professional job," Detective McCullough responded, and then added, "I'm not a profiler, but something just isn't right here. I haven't been able to pinpoint it yet, but I will. Whoever did this knows what we look for in a murder case."

Detective Scott Jones didn't flinch. He didn't even blink. He just nodded his head.

"Detective McCullough, I think I've found a few things that may be of interest," the young technician said.

Detective McCullough absorbed this new information with another twist of his lips.

"I think we found the murder weapon in the bathroom at the bottom of the hamper," the lab technician said, holding a plastic zip-lock baggie containing an ice pick.

"This is going to be easy to solve," Jones said smiling. "For Christ's sake, Scott!"

"Detective, we also found a couple of hairs that don't match the victim's in color."

"Listen up, gentlemen. Anything you find may that contain DNA--a hair, a hairbrush, a razor, a toothbrush, worn panties…

I mean anything! Bag it up for testing. Don't miss anything!"

"Pat, the bare bone of this case is that ice pick. Don't you think so?"

"No! I want everything, every lead, and every agent who was up in this house investigated, even the U.S. attorney."

The presence of the federal agents standing in front of Special Agent Yolanda Rivas' apartment started to draw a crowd. Neighbors started asking questions, and some of the news media were parked outside asking questions.

"Goddamnit, Scott! The last thing we need is to be in the spotlight. We don't need publicity at this moment. Get rid of them!"

"Pat, all we can do is keep them away from the crime scene. The victim was an agent with the CIA Special Crimes Unit, so you can't let your emotions get in the way of this one. What do we tell the media?"

"Nothing. Not until we have a positive lead. For now, none of us, and I mean none of us from homicide, will speak. If anyone leaks any information to the media, they will be looking for a new job after they get out of jail."

"I understand, and I'll instruct the rest of the guys. Pat, you as well as the rest of us in here know we won't be able to keep this quiet for long. We can't control the CIA."

"We're going to try our best." Detective McCullough's phone rang and he answered it immediately.

"Pat, it's the Commissioner. I know you're busy, but I need--"

"We'll be there soon, sir. What's the problem?"

The silence on the other end of the line was brief, and then the Commissioner said, "Problems, yes. I just got a call from the State's Attorney General, so we have problems."

"But--"

"We'll talk in person, Detective."

"I'm on my way."

Detectives McCullough and Jones stared at each other angrily. Receiving a call from the Commissioner could only mean three things: removal from the case, suspension, or desk duty. Whichever it was, it wasn't good at all.

Detectives McCullough and Jones sat at a conference table with Philadelphia Police Commissioner Tom Dancey, Assistant District Attorney Lee Berkson, and U.S. Attorney Charles Krinsky.

Commissioner Dancey said, "Let's get started, gentlemen." Then he looked at Detective McCullough. "Detectives, I'm going to make this short and simple. This department will not tolerate any disrespect from you or any detective on your watch towards the U.S. Attorney."

Detective McCullough stared at the Commissioner. His anger was growing by the second. "Sir, Detective Jones was only doing his job."

"I'm not done yet, Detective."

*This asshole is still a lap dog to the white man*, Detective McCullough thought to himself. *Look at him! The nigger hates his job, and the pathetic Mayor who tells him what to do. Yet he wants to call me in here just so he can look good.*

"Detective, after discussing this case with the U.S. Attorney and the Mayor's office, we decided to form a multi-jurisdictional task force to help solve this case fast. You two are to assist these fellows," Commissioner Dancey said, pointing to the CIA agents standing against the wall. "Do I make myself clear?"

"Sir, I mean no disrespect, hut Homicide has jurisdiction on this one." Detective McCullough wasn't going to bite his tongue on this one.

"Detective, if you have any problems following orders, you can be removed from this case."

"Sir, I'd rather be removed from this case. Conflict of interest will interfere with my performance."

"No problem. Request granted. How about you, Jones?"

"Me? No. I don't have any problems."

"Good!"

Detective Scott Jones was a ruthless asshole and a shame-less ass-kisser who had been nothing but a pushover in the department for the last twenty years.

"You are a weak coward, Scott! After this case is over, find yourself a new partner!" Detective McCullough said close to Jones' ear as he walked out of the Commissioner's office.

# CHAPTER 23
## "The Pick Up"

Inez and I lay in bed, tossing each other's salad and listening to the local news.

"Ma, I wish I could lie in bed with you all day long, but we must pick up our money from the Judge and Solo. But I promise you, I'll be here tonight to celebrate our come-up. I promise you, Ma."

I knew timing was everything to her plans. By 8:00 a.m. we were both ready to bounce. "Do you think they're gonna have the money?" I asked Inez, feeling cynical and jaded.

"They will. Trust me on this one, Ma. Those two perverts are on some 'Desperado' shit. They're not stupid. Two-mil ain't shit to them. This is bigger than me and you. Bigger than those two faggots. This is about saving them from a prison trip. This is about saving their careers. They don't want me to open a Pandora's box. Trust me; everyone involved in this kiddy porn ring is going down. So yes, they will have our money. I trust you, Ma. I just wish we could lie in bed all day. I can't get enough of you!"

I gave Inez one last kiss, sucking her lips until her nipples hardened.

I was quiet as Inez pulled her white Benz out of the parking garage and onto the busy downtown Philly streets. I continued to look out of the car window, basking in the day's experience and feeling happier than ever. The only regret I had was not telling Inez I was pregnant. Right then I had my mind on my money and my money on my mind. Maybe I would tell her tonight, or maybe I would just take my share of the money and disappear. I had to play this carefully, and I knew I wouldn't do it unless I had complete control of my emotions.

When Inez pulled in front of City Hall, my heart started beating faster. "Are you for this, Ma?" she asked.

"I think so." I raised one hand and brushed at my right cheek.

"At this point, there is no turning back," Inez said as she pulled out her cell phone and placed a call to Judge McCall.

"Hello?"

"Your Honor, do you have my money?"

My pussy twitched in my panties as I heard Inez bark her demands at the Judge.

"Are you listening, you little cunt?"

"I'm listening, Your Honor," Inez said with a smile.

"Suppose I don't have your money? Then what?"

"Then I would lose confidence in your abilities. Face it, Your Honor. I really don't need you any more. What I have is good enough to make me rich. Once the media gets wind of this tape, trust me, Your Honor, I will be on every TV show you can imagine. 'Good Morning America', 'Inside Edition', '20/20', and whatever other show offers me money. This is not a bluff. Don't have my money ready in five minutes, and you will see how bad things will get for you. That's a promise I can keep."

"I will kill—"

"Save it, Your Honor. Your verbal outbursts and threats don't impress me. All they do is make my pussy wet. Act stupid if you want to."

"What time are you supposed to come pick this money up?"

"Good question, but I already told you; just have my money ready when I get there in five minutes. Your Honor, the clock is ticking."

"You can't be serious! That's impossible!"

"Your Honor, my patience is running out!"

"You little cunts will pay for this!"

"We already paid when we shit in your nasty old mouth, you fucking pervert!"

"Fuck you, you little cunt! I--"

*"Click!"*

Inez shut the cell phone off and then threw it in a trashcan in front of City Hall.

As we entered the Criminal Justice Center, we both looked around to make sure nobody was following or watching us. We couldn't help but smile. The key to making this shit work was preparation, and Inez had been preparing for this day ever since she was ten years old. The CIA had taught her that great agents always prepared for every eventuality.

Once in front of Judge McCall's chambers, Inez knocked.

Softly, the Judge opened the door with an evil grin. I scanned his office for any unwanted company, and noticed two large black duffel bags by his desk. "Ladies, I guess our deal is sealed."

"Yes it is, Your Honor, and I'm glad you took us seriously, because I would hate to see what those booty niggas in prison would do to a wrinkled old white man who is responsible for filling those State prisons up with blacks and Latinos. A freak and a pervert like you probably would welcome being raped by some lifer with nothing to lose."

Inez handed me one of the duffel bags and took hold of the other. *Two million dollars!* The weight of the bag totally blew my mind!

"Aren't you ladies going to count your money?"

"No, Your Honor. No need for that. If and when we count our money and even one dollar is missing, you can kiss your ass good bye. However, I have faith in you," Inez said as we walked out of the Criminal Justice Center the same way we walked in; unnoticed.

By the time we drove to the National Bank on Market Street, Inez and I were both beside ourselves.

"My career in crime is burgeoning!" Inez said with a smile. "It seems I am now an extortionist as well as a notorious CIA agent."

"Sounds dangerous to me," I said sincerely.

Solo was waiting for us in his white Cadillac Escalade.

From a distance we spotted his pimped out ride sitting on twenty-inch custom chrome wheels. My face twitched into an awkward smile when Inez double-parked beside him, and I saw the hatred in his eyes. I guess being played by two females hurt more than being robbed by a nigga in a ski mask.

"Whatsamatta?" Inez asked, looking Solo straight in the eyes.

"You two bitches will some day pay for this! Why me? I've been nothing but good to you. Why me?"

"Listen here, punk boy! By the time I park my car, you'd better have my money. Save the crying games for someone else."

Inez found a parking spot three car away from Solo. We got out and walked to Solo's car, and got in, me in the front seat and Inez in the back. The inside of the Escalade was also pimped out. Leopard seats, color TV in the back, hundred-channel satellite dish on the roof, a GPS and telephone, and a sound system with enough power to host a North Philly block party.

"Why me?" Solo asked again, as if giving him an answer was going to make things better for him.

"Why not?" Inez responded, licking her lips.

"Because I been good to you two bitches, that's why!"

"Let's get this shit straight. This ain't no mothafucking Q&A session. Life has shined the harsh light of reality on your ass. Now, you can either give me my money here, or we can make this formal and go into your office. It really doesn't matter to me. But if by the time the meter for my parking space runs out, and I don't have my money, trust me, you won't be asking yourself, 'Why me?'"

Solo looked at me with a glint of irritation in his eyes. "Be easy, baby. I got your money."

"Tell me something I don't already, know, nigga!" Inez said from the back seat, leaning forward and pressing her lips against his ear.

"Whoa! Wait a sec! Slow down! I said you're gonna get your money. No need to rush!" He caught himself. He realized that he didn't have a fighting chance against two ruthless bitches whose mission was to destroy his ass.

"Nigga, you are on my time. Play stupid if you want to!" Inez said.

"I struggled for years to get where I'm today, and I'm supposed to just hand my money over to some bitch off the street after we fucked a few times? Bitch, is you crazy?"

"What choice do you have, faggot?" Inez spit out.

"Oh, I do have a choice. I don't have to give you jack-shit!"

In my peripheral vision I could see a couple of bank employees staring at Solo while he leaned forward and waved at them to get back to work. He then narrowed his eyes and faced Inez.

"You're absolutely right. You don't have to give me shit, but let me be clear. If you think this is a bluff, think again," Inez hissed.

I said nothing, looking idly out the window, checking the surroundings and making sure Solo wasn't trying to set us up.

"You see, bitch, I can get raw too. I really don't give a fuck if you send that DVD to every news station in the world. I don't give a fuck, bitch! Do you know who the fuck I am? Do you know who I'm related too? Bitch, sooner or later you will pay for this!"

Solo needed to be made an example of…the ultimate example. Taking his money wasn't going to be enough. Exposing his homosexual activities wasn't enough. Smashing his face wasn't enough. He needed to be taught a lesson, to never fuck with a mad woman on a mission. "Nigga, do you really think I care who you are or who you may be related to? I know who you are! A dick sucking, faggot ass nigga who runs around fucking under aged boys! I'm sure your mother will be pleased to hear that her only son is on his way to keep her company in prison. Maybe you can get there in time. You know lung cancer ain't no joke. Plus, those prison hospitals and nurses really don't give a fuck about a spic bitch who raped her own grandson! I'll bet they'd love to see her coughing up blood. You see, nigga, I done my homework on your ass! Now you got three minutes to come up with my money!"

"And if I don't?"

"If you don't, then I would have to tell you like Detective Alonzo said in 'Training Day': *'You wanna go home or you wanna go to jail?'* I don't give a fuck about you, nigga!" Inez's expression hardened. The message was clear.

"Bitch, you think you're slick! You think you could extort me, huh? Nobody fucks with me!"

"That's the difference. I'm somebody. Where the fuck is my money?"

"You just fucked your way into a lucky situation. Now you want to come up on a quick paid day. All you greedy whores are the same."

"Nigga, I'm running this show. I make the rules, so save the drama for your dying mother, and give me the loot!" Inez snapped.

"Fuck you!"

"*Fuck me!* Nigga, that's something you couldn't do right. My girl here got a better fuck game than you," Inez said pointing at me.

"Inez, this nigga's been talking too much. He can either give us the money, or we can bounce," I said.

I saw the nervous movement in Solo's eyes, the rapid breathing. "Whore, this is none of your fucking business!"

"Nigga, this is *all* my fucking business! It's been my business from day one! Us leaving here without our money is not acceptable!"

"What're you gonna do?"

I reached into my bag and pulled out a Glock and jammed the muzzle in Solo's face, smacking him solidly on the side of his mouth. "Nigga, this is not a game. Metal and bone don't go together."

Solo emitted an involuntary grunt.

"I'm gonna assume you got our money in the back, 'cause if you don't, my girl here is gonna unload her clip in your head, right here in this beautiful ride." Inez winked at me and smiled.

"Wait! Okay, just wait!" Solo got out of the front seat and walked over to another car parked in front of his. He popped the trunk, pulled out two large duffel bags and returned back to the Escalade, placing the bags on the driver's side. "Here's your money. Now give me my DVD," he said with fury in his eyes.

"Ma, I'm gonna check it out to make sure this nigga isn't playing no games with our money," Inez barked at me while I pointed my Glock directly at Solo's face. She unzipped the bag slowly and the stacks of cash were arranged in neat rows.

"It's all there," Solo said. "One million in each bag."

I felt my pussy dripping in my pants, and I looked at Inez and smiled.

"When we count it ourselves, I will make sure you get your DVD Trust me. I have no need for it now," Inez told him.

"Trust you! Bitch, the last time I trusted you I ended up being set up for two-mil!"

"Like I said, when we count our money, you will get your DVD. Have a nice day, faggot!"

Inez and I got out of his car and walked over to hers, only to find a Parking Authority officer writing her a ticket. We both laughed until we cried.

Inez parked in front of Philly Storage Center on Delaware Avenue, and looked at me with a sexy grind. "Baby, we're rich! Two million apiece! You can either store yours in here with mine, or you take your share and do whatever. It's your call."

I looked at her for a second and thought about all the possibilities and shit that could go wrong. *Fuck that! I'm keeping my own money with me. This bitch might rob me.* "Baby, girl, I'd rather keep my own shit. I don't believe in banks or storage."

"That's cool. Keep the two bags the Judge gave us, and I'll keep these. I'll be right back." Inez got out of the car and walked into the Storage Center. I sat in the front seat of her Benz, trying to come up with a good excuse to drive off with my two million and leave her alone.

After ten minutes, Inez returned with a key in her hand. "Listen, Ma. Hold on to this key. If anything happens to me, take the money and do whatever you want."

I sat there staring at her, not believing that she was willing to trust me with her money.

"Remember this, baby. Sometimes a person has to risk everything they love to achieve their goal. Life's defining moments are usually played under the shadows of doubts. After this case is over, we're taking a vacation together, anywhere you want to go, Ma. Now, where do you want me to drop you off?" Inez didn't wait for my response. She drove off smiling, stopping in front of the Painted Bride Art Center. When she parked, she looked me in the eyes and said, "I know you don't want me to know where you lay your head at night, and I respect that. Even though I have the capability to find out, I respect your personal space. I'll call you in two days." She leaned over and gave me the most passionate kiss I ever had. The bitch had me cumming in seconds.

I grabbed my two duffel bags and walked into the Painted Bride Art Center, sliding out the back door, which led to my apartment building. Once I was in my apartment, I lay in my bed not believing my luck. Financially, I was set, but I still had the reality of a child growing inside me, and time was against me. I only had a few weeks to make the biggest decision of my life, whether to keep this child or have an abortion.

# CHAPTER 24
### "It's Over, Fool"

Detective Scott Jones really didn't' give a fuck about how his partner, Patrick McCullough, felt. To him, this case was a career builder for everyone involved. *Fuck you, McCullough!* Jones thought to himself as he sat in his office waiting for the crime scene technician to finish lifting the fingerprints off the evidence they found in Special Agent Yolanda's apartment.

Under most circumstances, the Homicide Unit at the Round House was filled with murder suspects waiting to he questioned, some too young to be killers, and others too fucking stupid to even be considered criminals, but each one of them had their own ghetto tale of woe and unfulfilled ambitions. Today, for some reason, the Homicide Unit was almost empty. The special Task Force Unit, consisting of homicide detectives and CIA agents, all sat quietly. Word of the murder of Special Agent Yolanda Rivas spread fast. A fallen CIA agent naturally got the attention of the governor. Every unassigned CIA agent in the Tri-state was on his or her way to the Round House. By 5:00 p.m., there were sixty-five CIA agents, both men and women, waiting for the fingerprints.

"Sir, why don't we put the print card through the AFIS we've just installed at the CIA building? If the prints are on file they will return within two or three minutes," Special Agent Jasmine Rodriguez said to the U.S. Attorney, Charles Krinsky.

Homicide detectives were looking at her as if she was talking a foreign language.

"Excuse me! Can you explain what AFIS is to those of us who are not familiar with it?" Detective Jones asked.

"AFIS stands for 'Automatic Fingerprint Identification System'. This system has a larger database than the National Crime Identification System, and is faster. The CIA upgrades their technology every six months." Special Agent Rodriguez couldn't believe that homicide detectives weren't up on the latest technology for tracking down criminals.

On the third floor of the CIA building on Market Street, in a dark room at the end of a long corridor, the AFIS machine sat untouched. A black, bored looking girl was reading an *Essence* magazine.

"Eve, I need this run immediately," Special Agent Rodriguez said, handing her the fingerprint card. Within a minute, the AFIS machine started buzzing, indicating that there was a match. Special Agent Rodriguez grabbed the printout in the catch tray and looked at it. The photo she was looking at was of a clean-cut man with a small Afro. She immediately recognized him as Solo. His driver's license identified him as Brian Solomon, five-nine, one hundred and seventy-three pounds. He lived at 2025 North Cambria Street, North Philadelphia. The added information had his long history with the police.

Brian Solomon was a member of the violent street gang, *La Familia*, who were known in the city for their drug turf wars with the Latin Kings and the *Mara Salvatrchas*, better known as MS13. Special Agent Jasmine Rodriguez knew right there and then that Solo had to be dealt with and taken out of the equation. From looking at his rap sheet, she also noticed that Solo had been a paid witness for years for an unidentified homicide detective. If pressured a little, he would likely expose her extortion game, and she wasn't having it.

At the Round House, the CIA, the U.S. Attorney General and the city district attorney were preparing to hold a press conference. The CIA was taking the lead in the press conference, and they were basically declaring war on the city criminals and crooked politicians. By choice, the CIA used the same press conference to release indictments against unidentified city officials and local businessmen for child pornography.

Jari Medenia, a 'hood rat who cared for Solo's house in North Philly, answered the banging knocks.

Special Agents Rodriguez and Watts handed her the search warrant. "Federal warrant! Open the fucking door now!" Rodriguez announced.

Jari opened the door and stepped aside, smiling. She had grown up in North Philly under the infamous Mayor Frank Rizzo, so a little police aggression did not bother her.

Twenty CIA agents and three homicide detectives flooded into Solo's house and spread out. Since the Feds had gotten the search warrant, Special Agent Jasmine Rodriguez was assigned to lead the investigation.

"Agent Rodriguez!" The shout came from the master bedroom where a Latino federal agent stood next to a closet.

"What is it?" Rodriguez asked.

"Check this out." The Latino federal agent pointed down to the floor in the closet.

Rodriguez quickly knelt down and inspected the black case about four feet long by two foot high. She popped the lock and pulled the lid open. Lying on the bottom in black cut Styrofoam was a fully automatic AR-70 with ten fifty-round clips. Newspaper articles of Philadelphia's most recent cop killing were also in the case.

"Do you think this can he related?" Detective Jones asked, looking at the illegal firearm.

"I don't know."

"Officer Cuppinsky was killed with a Beretta AR-70."

"Have a gun residue test done right away." Agent Rodriguez looked over at detective Jones. "The Feds are not trying to make this a competition."

*What the fuck is going on here?* Solo thought as he watched two dozen police cars surrounding Cambria Street. Once one of his longtime neighbors spotted him and told him whose house the Feds had just raided, he didn't have to ask what was going on. *That fucking dirty bitch crossed me!* Eight more federal cars pulled up, as did the Channel 29 News.

"Nigga, if I was you, I'd hit ghost now. From the looks of things, it seems like you're in a world of trouble. What the fuck did you do?" his neighbor asked, enjoying the real life drama unfolding on Cambria Street.

*You crack head mothafucka, the only thing I did was fuck your faggot ass son in the ass for a few dollars.* "I ain't do shit, man!"

"Yeah, right!" the neighbor responded. *I bet that they have a reward out for him. I got to get that!* the old man thought to himself as he walked toward the CIA agents in front of Solo's house and pointed towards Solo.

"Mothafucka!" Solo shouted as he ran towards 5$^{th}$ Street. Once he made it to his hideout spot, he pulled his cell phone out and made a call to his connection in Camden, New Jersey.

"Hello?"

"*Primo* (cousin), what's happening?" Solo responded.

"Oh shit! *Primo*, where the fuck you been?"

"That's not important. Right now I'm on the run from the Feds."

"What! What happened?"

"Long story. I need your help. I need you to come and pick me up at my stash house. I got to get out of the city until I find out what's happening. Can you pick me up?"

"I don't have a ride right now, but my man can take me."

"No! No! I need you to come by yourself."

"Nigga, I told you I don't have a ride right now. My shit got impounded by the police last week."

"Can this man of yours be trusted?"

"Fuck, yeah!

"I'm telling you, Jay, I can't afford no slipups on this one. I'm not trying to end up in jail."

"Trust me, I got your back. My man is cool. I'll be there in a half hour."

Hot Tongue Jay was known in the streets of Camden as a rat--an informant for the CIA, and the man responsible for bringing down Mayor Milton Million. He was also known throughout the prison system in Camden as a boot licker, the nigga responsible for having all the major heads of the infamous prison gang, *La Familia* locked down or transferred out of state. This major rat had the desire to be known as "The Man", and he did whatever it took to reach his goal.

The streets were blazing with his name, but since the game was fucked up, rats were no longer a threat to the livelihood of a nigga's hustle. Being from Liberty Street gave this nigga an in-depth knowledge of who the real niggas were, and Lil' Ray-Ray was on top of the list. At the age of sixteen, Ray-Ray earned his street credibility as a gangster when he shot his next door neighbor with a .380 in the face when the neighbor caught him fucking his wife in the ass. After the shooting was considered a crime of passion by the authorities in, Camden, Ray-Ray was sent to juvie for six months. Once back in the streets, his name alone planted fear in niggas' hearts, and bitches were throwing their pussies at him just because they knew if their man got out of pocket, they would be dealt with by Ray-Ray.

A half-hour later, Solo was in the trunk of Ray-Ray's 2007 Benz, crossing the Ben Franklin Bridge on his way to Camden.

"Listen, if the Feds are looking for him, it won't be long before they go after his family. He can stay at my sister, Glady's crib for now. Trust me, he'll be safe there, you hear me?" Ray-Ray said as he parked his car in front of his sister's house. Ray-Ray also knew that if the nigga in the trunk was who his cousin claimed he was, he would probably be his next victim.

James Coben was a Philadelphia high rollers' attorney, who'd been on Brian Solomon's payroll since his early days as a street corner drug dealer down 8th and Butler. James Coben was best known in the legal circle for defaming police officers and prosecutors. He was a master in turning any case involving white officers into racially motivated incidents. He was insensitive towards the police and motivated by the dollars his clients paid him to stay out of prison.

He sat in his South Philadelphia office watching the local news when his cell phone sounded. He snatched it up and pressed it against his ear. "Who is it?" Whoever it was had his full attention. James listened in silence. His serious features turned into a smile. Five minutes later, he was able to speak. "My main man, this is not about pornography. No. This is about murder. Not just any murder. We are talking about the murder of a federal agent. Every cop and CIA agent in the city is on the hunt for you."

"What?"

"They got a federal warrant for your arrest. That's if they don't kill you first! Don't you watch the news?"

"Man, are you serious?"

"Listen to me, Solo. You can either surrender, or hold court in the street. You know my services are available to you. My fee will be twenty-five thousand to start with. I can try to buy you some time, but this is very real. They are out to kill you. So what are you going to do?"

"I ain't do it!"

"Who gives a fuck? I believe you, but they claim to have the murder weapon and hair that matches yours at the crime scene. From the looks of things, they have a solid case against you."

"I wanna turn myself in, but I have to take care of some business first."

"I will bring you in myself. Where are you staying?"

"I can't disclose that over the phone, but I will call you back in about an hour. James, believe me, I'm being set up for this!"

"Solo, as I stated, I really don't care if you did it or not. My only concern is keeping you alive."

*Yeah, and the cash money you stand to receive from me which probably won't get reported on your income tax.* His head was throbbing, his palms were sweating, and his legs wobbled. Solo was in emotional shock.

# Part Three

# CHAPTER 25
## "Fuck da Police"

Twenty-four hours after arriving back at my studio apartment, I still lay in bed hopelessly tangled in a ball, like a crackhead looking for a hit. I was undecided on to whether to call William or not. Damn it, I didn't expected him to have this kind of hold on me. I didn't anticipate him touching my heart. I didn't want to ever care for a man like this. In my gut-wrenching, mind-numbing ways, I could never be wifey to a man. I closed my eyes to block out the haunting image of William's face.

I finger-fucked myself, pretending I was riding William's dick. Even pretending was a good place to be. Alone in my apartment, I pulled out my bedroom toys. I lay on top of the sheet with my legs wide open, knees up and spread wide apart. "I want to feel your dick in my stomach, *Papi!*" I imagined myself telling William. The hard rubber dildo I was using was called the "Big Black Bomber", and believe me, it was big enough to hurt a bitch's pussy for days. The Big Black Bomber always hit its mark.

I closed my eyes, drew my knees up and worked the Black Bomber deeper and harder. I screamed, then turned on my side and pressed my fist into my pussy, turning it back and forth. My pussy ached. My pussy was wet, dripping like a water fountain.

I was hurt, but the pain was worth it. It was such a relief when I finally came.

The sheets smelled like pussy and sweat. I got up and changed the bed sheets. Then I went into the bathroom and took a nice cold shower. I got dressed and went down to Market Street to the Chinese nail spa and treated myself to a manicure and pedicure. Sitting in a chair in the spa, I felt a pain below my waist. *Stomach cramps! I've got to do something about this baby!*

"Hello, CIA office. How may I help you?"

"I have some information on the guy y'all are looking for in Philly. You know, the guy on the news? But first I have a question. Is there a reward for his arrest? Because I sure can use some help."

"Sir, I'm Special Agent Rodriguez, and I need to know where this suspect is immediately. Reward, yes, there is a reward. What is your name, sir?"

"I don't want to be mixed up in this shit. I mean, I'm not a snitch, I just want to help out. My name is not important."

"So how am I supposed to get the reward money to you?"

For a second the voice on the other line was caught off guard by the question. He had already broken the code of the streets by calling the CIA. What he failed to realize was that Agent Rodriguez was keeping him conversing on the line while she traced the location to where the call was coming from. When she got the location, she spoke again. "Listen, whenever you're ready to speak again, call the same number," she said, and hung up the phone.

Chino was upstairs in the living room ear hustling on Gladys' conversation with her brother, Ray-Ray, and decided to give Ray-Ray a little payback for the many times he had disrespected him. Chino hated Ray-Ray because he had fucked his sister, then had put his gun in her mouth when she started talking about being pregnant, making her abort the baby. But since Chino was pure pussy, he feared him. *Pay back is a mothafucka, nigga!* he thought as he picked up the phone and speed dialed the same number he had previously dialed.

"Agent Rodriguez speaking."

"I'm--"

"I know who you are. So, you decided to speak, huh?"

"My name is--"

"Hector Rivera, also known as Chino."

"How you know my name?"

*Some mothafuckas are stupid for real. How can he not know that his call could be traced?* "We are the CIA. We can find dirt on anyone we want, and if there is none, we can create it."

"Since you're the CIA, then you should know where I am."

"Yes, I know where you're calling from. Let me ask you a question. How many people are in the house besides you? Are there any weapons in the house?"

"I don't know about any weapons, but there's three people

in the house, and I'm about to get the fuck out of here. I don't want any part of this shit. So, when and where can I get my reward money?"

"I'll be in touch with you. Trust me; I know where to find you."

Ray-Ray was returning to his sister, Gladys' house when he noticed a shit load of DEA agents, Camden cops and CIA agents surrounding his sister's crib, kicking in the front door. He reached under the front seat of his car and pulled out a Uzi with a banana clip. "Fuck da Police! he yelled over the old classic Hip Hop tune from Dr. Dre and Snoop Dogg. "It's just a 187 on a undercover cop!" His adrenaline was pumping fast. He felt like he had uncanny strength, and he was ready to die like Biggie Smalls.

He exited his car undetected, sucked in some air, and opened fire as the cops were about to enter his sister's house. As the Cops and agents scrambled over each other, Ray-Ray reloaded and squeezed off some more rounds, lighting their asses up like it was the Fourth of July.

*"Blaow! Blaow! Blaow! Blaow! Blaow! Blaow!"*

Instinctively, inside the house, Gladys and Solo ran for cover, and were making their getaway through the basement door that led to an alleyway.

"Stop! Police!" two CIA agents yelled, shooting at them.

They kept running until they thought they were safe. Solo was just following Gladys' lead. She hid under a pile of trash. The stench crawled into her nose.

Sirens shattered the contaminated air of the streets of Camden. Footsteps and radio static could be heard. A young federal agent had them trapped. He aimed for her head when he saw Gladys. "Let me see your hands! Now!" They were both frozen for a split second. The CIA agent blinked when a rat scrambled over his leg, giving Gladys enough time to pull her nine out, blasting him in his mouth and knocking his teeth out of his skull like splinters. Gladys wasn't a gunslinger: she was working out of pure fear. She stood over the young CIA agent and shot him pointblank in the jaw. Blood trickled from his mouth. She kicked him in the face hard enough to ensure that that he was dead.

"They're gonna want to nail me for this shit here," Solo said as he and Gladys took a taxi back to Philly.

Gladys took a breath, closed her eyes. "I don't give a fuck about what you think they're going to do to you! My brother just got killed for trying to help you, nigga!"

"I didn't ask him to help me. I asked my cousin."

"You're right, nigga!"

Oh, Christ…"

"Christ, my ass!" Gladys whispered. She slid out of the taxi on Delaware Avenue, almost laughing.

# CHAPTER 26
## "Dead or Alive"

I sat in the Chinese spa staring at the flat screen TV in the center of the room and was amazed. This was definitely one for my scrapbook.

> *"We are at the scene of a double shooting on Delaware Avenue. Philadelphia police are not saying much, but both victims are believed to be dead: two males, one African American and one Hispanic. The CIA has taken over the crime scene. Reliable sources within the department have informed us that one of the suspects in the taxi may be Philadelphia's most wanted murder suspect, Brian Solomon. Police and CIA agents are not speaking to the media at this time. Fox 29 News will remain at the scene, covering it minute by minute as this story unfolds. This is David Schratwieser, for Fox 29 News."*

The spa wasn't too far from Delaware Avenue, so I decided to take a walk down to the crime scene and stand with the rest of the spectators behind the yellow tape.

A black woman screamed out as she was held by a police officer, "That's my husband! Please let me see my husband!"

In the front passenger seat I could see Solo slumped over.

The spectators were all trying to get a peek of Philly's most wanted man. For some reason, crime scenes always drew a large crowd of people who wanted only to witness the real drama, and play a small part in Philadelphia's most exciting news. We saw it on the evening news, we read about it in the newspaper, but there was nothing more fascinating than seeing it live in real time. Watching the medical examiner, the homicide detectives and the coroner doing their trades had always turned me on.

I smiled when I spotted Inez in her blue jacket with yellow letters. I wanted to call her over, but decided against it for personal reasons.

Inez winked at me, and walked over to me. "What are you doing here?" she asked me, looking round to ensure that no one was ear hustling in on her conversation.

"I was getting my nails done and saw it on the local news, and decided to walk down her. What happened?"

"Somebody slumped Solo. The whole car is drenched in blood. Whoever shot him made sure he was dead. They shot him behind the right ear, execution style. There's blood and brain matter all over the place. The driver was shot once in the temple."

"So, does this mean the case against Solo and the Judge is closed?" I asked her for the sake of conversation.

"No. It just means we have one less pervert to arrest. But the Judge is going down tomorrow. After this, we're going on a vacation," Inez said as she headed back towards the taxi.

I really didn't trust anyone, and although Inez had proven her loyalty to me, I still didn't trust her. I had a bad feeling that some bullshit was about to jump off behind Solo being found dead in a taxi. The media was already speculating that Federal Agent Yolanda Rivas may have been corrupt and involved in a romantic affair with Solo. Usually, the CIA tried to keep the shooting of one of their own under wraps until they had all the facts or an arrest had been made. It was clear that someone was feeding the media. The uglier it was, the more the media liked it. Despite this carefully orchestrated urban fiction nightmare, I was no match for Inez. If shit went sideways for her, the political whores and cops were going to take her side. Plus, I seen the bitch go postal.

*Fuck her! I got more than I anticipated out of this whole deal.* It sounded pathetic, but Inez needed to understand that the whole world--or my world--didn't revolve around her. With so much at stake, she wasn't giving me much assurance about anything, so I had to look out for myself.

When I got home, my mind was already made up. I took out fifty thousand and tucked it in my bag, then I took the rest of my money and headed back out the door. The whole thing would have been uncomfortable for anybody else, but for me it was like a blessing from the sky. *The bitch really had to be stupid to think she couldn't be gotten,* I thought to myself as I walked into the Philly Storage Center with the key that held Inez's future.

The old black man escorted me to Inez's rented space and disappeared into a side office. My gut turned into a bunch of knots. For a minute I thought about the dirty shit I was about to do, but thought, *Fuck it! If the bitch was stupid enough to give me the keys to her stash, then she needed to be taken for all she was worth.*

At first my eyes needed to adjust to the darkness in the room. Once I found the light switch and the lights came on, my jaw almost hit the floor. The storage room was stacked with boxes. My curiosity got the best of me. I flipped the lid on one of the boxes, and discovered plastic bags containing bundles of ecstasy pills. Some of the boxes contained bricks of weed. I would never have thought that Inez was into drugs. *You really can't tell what a mothafucka has in their closet until you look.*

I opened the two duffel bags to check that the money was there, then closed them and threw them over my shoulder and walked out of the storage room with a wet pussy and a smile. Having money always made my pussy wet. I tried to tell myself that I couldn't spend a lot of time worrying about Inez and her homicidal tendencies.

Luckily for me, within three minutes of standing in front of the Philly Storage Center, I flagged down a taxi driver who was willing to take me to my next destination, the Holy Sepulchre Cemetery in Cheltenham. I was so excited that I gave the driver a one hundred-dollar bill for a ten-dollar ride. The cemetery was closed, but the caretaker was willing to allow me to enter for the right price.

"Miss, we're closed!"

"Listen, I must see my mother, please!"

"I could lose my job."

"But you won't."

"How can you be so sure of that?" the caretaker asked, staring at my ass.

"I'll make it worth your while," I said, reaching for his zipper. I pulled out his dick and got on my knees, blowing kisses on the head of his dick. Old boy was working with something. I had him near ejaculation within five minutes. When I thought he was about to bust, I took him out of my mouth and jerked him off. "When was the last time you had some good ass?" I asked him, still jerking him off. "If you let me see my mother's gravesite, I'll make sure you enjoy a nice piece of ass." I got up off my knees, went into my bag and pulled out a stack. "There's one thousand dollars. Now, can I see my mother's gravesite?"

"Sure! Sure! Take your time!"

And my time I took. Once I was sure the caretaker wasn't following me, I dug a hole on the right side of Mrs. Penny's tombstone with a portable shovel I had managed to take from the caretaker's office. I dug deep enough to stash all four duffel bags.

"Mrs. Penny, I'm sorry, but his is the only safe place I could think of. So much has happened in these last few weeks since I visited you. I have so much to share with you, and I don't know where to begin. Please don't be mad at me."

I couldn't contain my tears as I filled in the hole. I was still wrestling with demons from my past. I knew doublecrossing Inez could lead to some real intrigue, but I was prepared to face the drama. After all, I did have two bodies under my belt.

For the next few hours, I sat by Mrs. Penny's gravesite and poured my heart out to her:

"Mrs. Penny, I don't know what to do about this baby. I don't know how to be a mother. What if I turn out to be like Sonia? As much as I want to find my daughter, I'm scared." It was two in the morning when I decided to head back home.

On the way out of the cemetery, the caretaker stood in my path and said, "Young lady, didn't you promise me something extra?"

"Old head, here is another thousand dollars, enough for you to buy yourself some young tender ass. I'll be back in a few days to bring my mother flowers, same time." I knew that an extra thousand dollars would make the old man forget about some ass.

"No problem, as long as you're willing to pay the same price," the old man said with a perverted smile.

I wasn't sure if he was taking about another two thousand dollars, or the quick head job I had given him. Whatever he meant, I'd deal with it when the time came. I left the cemetery without the caretaker noticing that I wasn't carrying the bags I had over my shoulders when I first arrived.

Back in my apartment, I gathered all of my papers, Birth Certificate and ID card. I didn't even bother to pack my clothes. For what? I had enough money to buy a brand new wardrobe and then some. I made sure I didn't leave behind anything that could identify me. Taking one more look around the apartment

I was satisfied. I wrote a note and placed five hundred dollars in an envelope, sealed it and place it under the landlord's door. Once outside, I pulled my cell phone out and called William. The phone rang about eight times before he answered.

"Hello?"

"William?"

"Speaking. Who's this?"

I stood silent for several seconds before I spoke again. "It's me, Mita."

"Damn, girl! Where have you been? I haven't heard from you in a while. I was starting to get worried."

"Are you mad at me, William?"

"Baby, I have no reason to be mad at you."

"I feel better now."

"So, what made you call me at this time?"

"I'm lonely and horny. Plus, I miss you."

"Is that right?"

"Yeah."

"So why don't you let me come pick you up and we can spend the rest of the morning taking care of your problems? I'm off today."

"Give me your address. I'll come over and bring you some breakfast."

"I live at 2031 North American Street. You sure you don't want me to come pick you up?"

"I'm a big girl. I know my way around the city. I'll see you in about a half hour," I said in my sweet voice, visualizing

William's dick being rock hard.

When I arrived at William's house, he was waiting for me butt ass naked. I shivered all over seeming his big dick standing like a flagpole. My nipples sprang up as he gently placed his hand under my shirt and began to caress one of my breasts.

"Come on. Let's go into the bedroom. I'm really not that hungry. We can eat breakfast later," William murmured into my ear.

On the bed he buried his face between my lush tits and began finger fucking my wet pussy. Already he could smell the wetness and feel the heat rising from between my thighs. He quickly pulled my thongs down to my ankles, coaxing me to raise first one leg and then the other and kick my thong off.

"Bend over and grab your ankles," he instructed me in a real sexy voice.

My graceful thighs parted automatically, baring the inside of my pink pussy. "What... what are you going to do?"

"I'm going to eat your asshole," William replied.

"Oh!" I replied.

There was a brief silence. William slowly got on his knees, leaned forward and buried his face between my legs. His tongue shot directly into my asshole until he stabbed the tip of his tongue deep inside of me.

"Nnnngggggggg!" I screamed. I gripped my ankles tightly. My whole body went rigid in reaction to what his tongue was doing to my fully exposed asshole.

William spread my ass cheeks wide holding them open,

then began to work his tongue in little circles, fluttering it wildly, flicking it back and forth.

"Ooooooohhhhhhhh," I moaned, my voice hoarse and out of control.

William removed his tongue from my ass and began sucking my clit. I felt the big orgasm rising inside me. I needed to come now!

"Goddamn, baby!" William muttered, desperately taking his rock hard dick in his hand and slowly driving it up in my pussy.

I tightened my pussy muscles, wanting to feel every inch of his dick. He drove his whole dick in me all the way to the hilt. "Aaaaaahhhhhhhh," I screamed as he fucked the shit out of me. His long fat dick flashed mercilessly in and out of my wet pussy, glistening with my juices. My tits bounced and swelled. "Oh! Oh, shit! Fuck the shit out of me, nigga! Fuck me in the ass! Make me love you, nigga!"

"This pussy is too good, baby!" William said as he pulled his dick out of my dripping pussy and started rubbing it up and down the crack of my ass. "Oooohhhh...Shit!" he shrieked as he pushed the head of his dick into my tight ass.

"It hurts! Please be careful, *Papi*!"

"Just try and relax. Try to loosen up for me," William groaned loudly, and with all his strength, he rammed his rock hard dick as far up in my ass as it would go, determined to fill my asshole with his cum.

My ass tightened, milking him greedily as he began to

cum. As soon as he pulled out of me, I collapsed on the floor and turned on my stomach.

William lay on top of me and began sucking my ass cheeks. "Damn, baby! That's the best piece of ass I ever had!"

I smiled, because I knew my shit was good. As I lay on the floor, my body still throbbed and tingled with the after effects of the hardcore ass fucking William had just given me. Lying next to him on the floor, I was wondering if this was the right time to tell him that I was pregnant. "William, we need to talk about something important," I said as he lay next to me with his soft long dick rubbing on my leg.

"What? You got any news on your daughter?"

"Naw. It's about us... me and you."

"What about us?" There was a sudden deathly silence as we both stared at each other.

"Listen, William. I'm pregnant. You're the only person I've been fucking raw. I understand if you have any doubts, but trust me, it's yours." I wasn't about to play any games. Now it was up to him to accept it or not.

"Damn, baby! Are you going to keep it?"

"I haven't decided yet."

"Fuck you mean you haven't decide yet?" William said angrily.

"Like I said, I haven't decided yet."

"Well, when you decide what you're going to do, let me know so I can be aware." William got up off the floor and gave me a hateful look as he walked into the bathroom.

I began to cry. "William, wait! I didn't mean it that way. I'm just confused right now."

He walked toward me and gave me a hug. "Listen. If the baby is mine, then I want the opportunity to man up to my responsibility. Am I asking for too much?"

"No. I'm just scared."

"You don't have to be scared. I got your back, baby." He had a stern look like he had an attitude, but I knew he was pussy whipped to the point of no return. He grabbed his soap, washcloth and towel and led me to his shower.

For the first time in my life, I felt secure in the company of a man.

"William, why don't we move out of this city and settle down somewhere? I have enough money to take care of us. I mean, we could start our own business," I said as he rubbed my back with the washcloth.

"Baby, I'm a man. Therefore, I do what real men do. I work and take care of my responsibilities."

"I know, *Papi,* but I'm in a position where I can take care of us for a while. Let's just say that I have a couple of million dollars within my reach."

"What? You rob a bank?"

"Something like that," I replied in a joking manner.

"Are you serious?"

"No… I mean yes, I'm serious. No, I didn't rob a bank, but I do have enough money to take care of us. I'll give you until Saturday to decide. After that, I must bounce from the city. If I don't, I'm gonna be wanted dead or alive."

"I want to know what's going on. Are you in some kind of danger?"

"No. The story is too long. I just need your answer by Saturday morning."

This has been the biggest and most important decision I would ever make in my life. It would be life altering, not only for me and my unborn child, but for anyone who decided to fuck with me.

# CHAPTER 27
## "Judgment Day"

*A vicious serial rapist was bad enough,* Agent Rodriguez thought. *But a vicious rapist in possession of little girls and boys was literally an urban nightmare...* her nightmare. To her, this case was personal, and for her to gain her humanity back, she needed to close this case.

Finally, she moved her hand as if she was waving for everyone's attention and said, "Okay, today we are serving indictments on some very influential people. This mission must be carried out quickly before the media gets wind of it."

Agent Thomas, a twenty year veteran of the CIA, asked, "How much time do we have, and how many targets are we hitting?"

"We don't have much time. With everything that's been happening in the last few days, I wouldn't be surprised if the media is already waiting for us outside. Once those assholes latch on, this story will be sensationalized. I don't want our suspects to be tipped off. This is a child pornography ring case, but our suspects are a city judge and a business owner in North Philadelphia. One of the suspects already met his Maker just yesterday. Yes, Agent Rivas' killer was our third suspect in this ease."

U.S. Attorney Charles Krinsky looked at Agent Rodriguez with raised brows. "This is a very important case for my office. Our victims are all underage. The families of the victims are going to be shocked by these arrests once they found out. Some may not be receptive of the media because of embarrassment; others will run to the media to make a public appeal for justice. That seems to be the thing these days. Right now, the community is feuding with the police, so there is no room for any fuck ups."

The room was silent for a few minutes, and then Agent Rodriguez stirred. "We have a job to do! We are the CIA, and I don't give a damn about how the community feels toward law and order," she said. "At the end of the day, when these perverts molest their children, we are the ones they call, so their emotional feelings towards us don't really matter to me. Am I the only one who feels this way?"

"No. And I'm sure everyone in this room feels the same way," U.S. Attorney Charles Krinsky said. "Good! Let's get to work."

Agent Jasmine Rodriguez wanted to make these arrests quickly before noon, because she didn't want to miss the meeting she had agreed to attend with the lady who might be her mother. All week she had been working overtime, tightening up all the loose ends to this case. She was hoping that the secret she had carried with her for as long as she could remember could be erased. She needed to find her parents. She needed answers.

Judge Larry McCall arrived at his chambers early, worried about the tip he had just received. *Goddamn, how could this be*

*happening to me? I'm not going to prison.* He was undecided on whether to call his attorney, or administrate justice on his own. After all, he was one of the most vicious judges in the city.

As Judge McCall sat at his desk contemplating his next move, the dark shadow dressed in black placed his hand over the Judge's shoulder in a not-so-gentle fashion. When he turned, he was face to face with a brown skinned black man who was wearing a skullcap. "What do you want?" Judge McCall asked.

"Nothing," the black man replied as his fingers stabbed into the judge's ribcage like a knife.

Crippling pain ran down the Judge's left side. He tried to scream and fight, but he couldn't move.

The black man moved his hands to the Judge's balls. He squeezed until the Judge's eyes rolled back. With his other hand he snapped the Judge's right shoulder out of its socket. He bent down and looked at the Judge with a smile, "So, you like fucking little innocent boys and girls?" His tone was gentle. Not waiting for a response, he punched the Judge in the mouth, knocking his teeth out.

The Judge's eyes bulged. *Oh God! Please don't let this nigger kill me! I don't want to die like an animal! Oh God! Please don't let me die!* The pain was too much for him to handle. It shut down every nerve in his body. Judge McCall tried to open his mouth to scream, but his voice was paralyzed.

The black man smiled as if he was enjoying himself watching the Judge suffer. "Your Honor, today is Judgment Day, and you must pay for all your sins. Tell God I say hi!"

*"...And He hath given it to be furbished, that it may be handled: this sword is sharpened, and it is furbished to give it into the hand of the slayer..."* the black man said as he flipped the Judge on his stomach spread-eagle, and pulled his pants down to his ankles. He grabbed the gavel from off of the desk and shoved it up the Judge's ass.

*Lady Justice would be happy to hear that justice had been serve equally amongst the rich and the poor,* the black man thought to himself as he squeezed the pressure points on either side of the Judge's head. When the Judge crumpled into a ball, the black man pulled a long, thin nylon rope from his back pocket and tied it tightly around the Judge's neck. The Judge started bucking against the rope, but he wasn't much of a match for the black man. He was suffocating; he needed oxygen.

The Judge's body jumped around like an epileptic. Once he stopped kicking and jumping, the black man threw the nylon rope over the ceiling fan and lifted the Judge's nasty body up.

The Judge hung from the ceiling fan overlooking the skyline of downtown Philadelphia with the same gavel he had used to administer justice to countless of society's lowlifes sticking out of his ass.

The man slid out of the Judge's chambers undetected, the same way he entered, through the side door of the chambers. Even as he saw the CIA agent entering the Criminal Justice Center, the black man knew that justice had already been served. He reported to his regular duties as a custodial maintenance employee on the first floor of the Criminal Justice Center, prepared to fulfill yet another day of work.

Agent Rodriguez stood inside Judge McCall's chambers, staring at the scene of carnage covered in blood. She could smell the Judge's shit that was dripping down his legs. "Well, I guess someone else gave the good old Judge a one way ticket to hell!" She conjured up a smile when she saw the unspoken hanging from the ceiling.

"This is the second suspect connected to this case that we lost in the last two days," U.S. Attorney Charles Krinsky said.

"It looks personal, doesn't it? The hunter has become the hunted," Agent Rodriguez said.

Charles Krinsky sent her a wry look. "Yeah, the hunter's been hunted, but as a cop, it's my job to seek justice. Whoever did this is putting my case on the line," he said with a tinge of bitterness in his voice.

"Sometimes justice is served in strange ways. We still got another suspect to arrest, so the spotlight is still on you," Agent Rodriguez blared out with a smile.

"This isn't about the spotlight, this is about justice!" Charles said, trying to maintain his composure. The fact was that he was banking on this case to announce his candidacy for Governor of Pennsylvania.

"Justice, huh?"

"That's my main goal in this case. I don't have any tolerance for politics."

*Cracker, please! Who the fuck do you think you're fooling?*

*Politics! It's written all over your pale ass face!* "Every high profile case is built on some kind of politics."

"Agent Rodriguez, let me make myself clear. I took an oath to protect the people of Pennsylvania from scumbags such as our suspects, and I do my job well. My office's conviction rate is the best in the nation, and we don't make deals! I get the job done. For me, politics is nothing but a game." Charles Krinsky wasn't sure if he was trying to convince Agent Rodriguez or himself of the bullshit he was saying.

"Tell me this, sir. When was the last time a U.S. Attorney has been on an arrest mission?"

For a second Charles didn't know whether to answer the question or change the subject. It was clear that Agent Rodriguez was much smarter than she looked. *Bitch, don't you recognize that I have the power to fire your ass? I have the power to have your ass on public assistance for the rest of your pretty life. You don't want to fuck with me on this one.* "I've been on plenty of missions since taking this post," he said with anger in his voice.

"Wait a minute, buddy! I play for the same team you play for, so don't get mad at me. I'm just saying that some things are going to happen regardless of what we do. Sometimes we can't prevent something from happening, and sometimes we can. It's part of the job."

"I guess I have to get used to it," he said slowly.

"Charles, let's go. The uniforms will take care of the crime scene."

"Yeah, yeah."

"We can't ever expect miracles in these kind of cases."

"Shit!"

"Charles, just remember that we're on the same side of the law, okay?" Agent Rodriguez said.

"Right. So, what now?"

Agent Rodriguez smiled, then said, "Let's go arrest the last pervert in this case." She was feeling herself because things were occurring the way she had planned. Either way, time wasn't on her side. For some reason today, time seemed to be moving slowly for her. She was anxious to close this case so she could meet with her latest potential, Internet stranger. After all the drama the week had dealt her, she really didn't expect to relax until Saturday.

Charles Krinsky looked at her with a hateful stare. She frowned at him, then started the dark unmarked car and began maneuvering it down Broad Street towards North Philly. From the backseat, Charles said, "I wonder what kind of surprise this suspect will have for us?"

"I hate surprises, because most of the times in missions like this, people die," Agent Rodriguez said, looking at the U.S. Attorney through the rear view mirror.

CIA helicopters descended on Erie Avenue. Two dozen CIA agents surrounded El Bodegero Grocery Store. The drug dealers on the block scattered out of sight and whispered among themselves, pointing at the store. It was no secret that many of the neighborhood hot-in-the-pants young girls had been molested by El Bodegero.

Agent Rodriguez moved in immediately, deftly drawing her weapon as she walked through the doors of the store. The smell of young pussy permeated her nostrils as she breathed deeply.

Each CIA agent had their weapons drawn, ready to fulfill their oaths.

Charles Krinsky was growing crazy with worry, frustration and disgust. Realizing that he was being observed by the other CIA agents, he had to control himself from snapping out. For that would have demonstrated that he was still at odds with Agent Rodriguez.

"Goddamn!" El Bodegero muttered hungrily. Taking his hard dick in one hand, he scrambled closer on his knees, looking his latest victim in the eyes. She was lying naked on her back, her brown glossy eyes staring into the camera lens that El Bodegero had set up in the back room of his store. The power welled within him, and his body was stirring and hardening as her brown eyes filled with terror. Every moment... every second counted. El Bodegero was enjoying the feeling he felt inside himself; the feeling that he could bend any little girl or boy to his will. This feeling had him feeling invincible.

His dick was so hard that he had to jerk off on the girl's face. He could hear his own breath coming fast. His rigid legs were trembling. He wanted--he needed to fuck this girl. He needed to be up in her innocent wound, to thrust, to pound, but he forced himself to remain still as he emptied his balls in spasms of pleasure. His teeth gritted like a monster's as he squeezed his dick.

"Wow, that's, uh...uh..." Charles couldn't talk.

Every CIA agent in the room wanted to make the arrest fast, but Agent Rodriguez was the head bitch in charge, and she wasn't ready. She wanted a solid case.

"Agent Rodriguez, what are we waiting for to arrest this pervert?" Charles Krinsky whispered, not hiding the anger in his voice.

There was a brief silence, and then Agent Rodriguez said, "Sometimes things have to get worse before they get better. If we want to put this bastard away for life, we need more evidence."

"What the fuck is that supposed to mean?"

"Sir, you may be the U.S. Attorney, but we are the ones out here day and night, not you. So fall back and let us do our job. We are the best at what we do. And remember that we're on the same side of the law," Agent Rodriguez said in a cold, implacable, evil voice.

"Are we here to help, Agent Rodriguez? The best thing you could do for me is to arrest this suspect. Why do you keep tying to carry all this alone? Let me help!" Charles sounded frustrated.

"You can help by letting me do my job. I don't need to be chaperoned by you." She hoped she was getting through this asshole who had been in the way since day one. She was wishing for things to turn violent so she could see what this asshole was made of. She knew he wasn't cut out for this kind of work, and she was willing to test him and call his bluff.

Charles' fingers tightened, and for a few seconds he wasn't sure if he should hit her below the waistline with a cheap shot to let her know and remind her of who she really was in this field. Finally, he said in a deliberate evil tone, "Agent Rodriguez, you, out of everyone in this room, should know what that girl is going through at this moment!"

Rodriguez stared at him, not as surprised as she wished she could be. All her life she had been hearing how lucky she was to have made it out of the foster care system. "You're right, I know what that girl is going through! That's why I'm in charge, so fall the fuck back!" *Cracker, don't you know I will blow your head off right here on the spot?* she said to herself, giving Charles a sinister look.

"It hurts!" the girl panted.

EL Bodegero had been through this many times before. "Just try and relax. I'ma give you an extra hundred dollars. Try to open yourself up for me." He could feel her pussy fighting back against his dick, and he loved that feeling. The girl's entire body was literally shaking. As soon as his dick head started up inside of her tender depths, it was all the same; fear and resistance.

"Aaaaaahhhhhhhh!" the girl screamed in pain.

"Ooohhhh... shit!" El Bodegero shrieked when he felt a piece of metal on the back of his head.

"If you move one inch, you will die!" Agent Rodriguez

said, hoping El Bodegero would do otherwise.

One of the other CIA agents grabbed El Bodegero by the hair and began to beat him over the head with his weapon. "Don't resist me, motherfucker!" the agent shouted.

"Gilberto Colon, you are under arrest for rape, kidnapping and sexual molestation of a minor. You have the right to remain silent. You have the right to have an attorney. If you can't afford one, the State will provide one for you. Do you understand these rights, sir?" Agent Rodriguez knew El Bodegero understood, but still she needed to run down the standard CIA bullshit just in case some hot shot attorney wanted to claim that his client wasn't read his rights.

The scene was disturbing. The young girl couldn't have been no more then fourteen years old. From the fear in her eyes, Agent Rodriguez cold see that the kid was definitely innocent, without a clue of the cruel reality which surrounded her.

The four male CIA agents in the room were angry and aggressive. They were a captive audience. They were impatient and they wanted to T.O.S. (terminate on sight) El Bodegero.

For the next few seconds, Agent Rodriguez and Charles Krinsky stared at El Bodegero, shaking their head back and forth.

"Get the fuck up, you perverted coward! You're going to 'Booty Land' where convicts with big dicks will be glad to fuck you!" Agent Rodriguez said close to El Bodegero's ear.

When he tried to rise, she planted her right knee in his balls, sending him back to the floor on his face.

"That's enough, Agent Rodriguez!" Charles Krinsky said.

"Or what? You going to bring me up on charges for disobeying your orders?" she said as she put the heel of her boot to the backside of El Bodegero. "How do you like it, you pervert?" she asked. "Fear! Isn't that what you like to see in those little girls and boys? That's why I'm arresting your ass. I'm very impressed with your video operation." Agent Rodriguez kicked him one more time straight in the ass, and El Bodegero fell over onto his side.

The other CIA agents lifted El Bodegero up from the floor and cuffed him from behind, but ass naked.

"Bring him outside! You're going to be Philly's most famous child molester. Believe me; your fans in prison are waiting."

Once outside, Charles Krinsky was on cloud nine when he saw the media.

"Sir, this is CNN. Can you please brief us on the arrest of this suspect?" the blonde reporter said, sticking a microphone in the face of Charles Krinsky.

"Our suspect had been under investigation for a year now for child pornography. We believe that he is the leader of a national ring that deals in child pornography over the Internet. My office will be having a press conference as soon as we get all the facts and details together. Thank you."

"Sir, is this case connected to the murder of the Honorable Judge McCall? Reliable sources are saying that it is. Can you tell us?" one local reporter asked.

"No comment!"

Suddenly, the reporters turned their attention toward the young girl who was being led to an unmarked CIA car with a CIA jacket over her head.

Agent Rodriguez looked around and locked eyes with Charles Krinsky, who seemed to be enjoying his audience; the media.

"Sir, it's been rumored that you are thinking about making a run for the governor's office. Is that true?"

Charles smiled and turned towards the reporter. "It's a possibility. Right now, I'm here to ensure the people of this great city that we will not tolerate anyone abusing our children."

Agent Rodriguez smiled and flipped her middle finger at Charles as she got into her car.

# CHAPTER 28
## "I'll Be There"

William dropped me off on the corner of American and Lehigh Avenue, about half a block from Isla Verde Restaurant. I knew the area well enough. As a child I used to play down by the old train tracks, back when American and Lehigh Avenue were nothing but train tracks. I was attending Roberto Clemente Middle school at the time, and cutting through the train tracks was the short way to school. Those were the bad years of my life.

*Twenty-five minutes until meeting time.*

I headed down American Street into an area heavily occupied by the brainchild of Ray Pastrana, Plaza Americana. This community shopping mall was owned and operated by one man, who in the early eighties, bought up a bunch of property in North Philadelphia when it was affordable. Fast forward to 2009, and Ray Pastrana is the Donald Trump of American and Lehigh.

My heart pounded on my chest walls like a long dick nigga pounding on some tight ass, juicy pussy. Could she be my daughter? Would she be there?

I caught my reflection in the window of Cousin Food Market, and couldn't help but notice that I looked good... too good for myself. From where I stood inside the food market I could see directly into Isla Verde. I decided to stay inside the food market because I wanted to be undetected. Shit, as far as I was concerned, this shit might be a setup. I'm down with the game. Some of these dirty niggas out here be playing, putting adds on My Space and Craig's List hoping to catch themselves a quick vic.

I kept my eyes directly on the front door of Isla Verde. I felt tense. Too much was happening and to fucking fast.

*Jasmine wasn't there yet!* My legs were shaking uncontrollably. I've never been so scared in my entire life, like I was today. I wondered if I should just bounce now while I was ahead. "What if indeed she was?" I whispered to myself. Trembling with terror and adrenaline, I wasn't prepared to deal with yet another letdown, but I had no other choice but to wait.

I bought an orange juice, wrapped my sweet lips around the bottle and waited for what seemed like an eternity.

Ten minutes later, I noticed a familiar car, and my eyes couldn't believe what they were seeing. I wanted to scream. I wanted to run out of Cousin Food Market, and just run until I dropped dead. But my legs for some reason wouldn't obey my commands. I looked at the person who got out off the car, and froze in fear.

"Hell no! No! No! Fuck, no! I'm seeing shit! This can't be real!" I yelled out. Panic flared through my body. "Ah, Inez--" I could feel the pain in the center of my chest and the bitter agony in my voice. The more I stared at her, the more I struggled to breathe. I felt like I was being choked. I felt defeated. *This can't be real!* I closed my eyes. *This shit is crazy! How can I turn such a devastating experience into some sort of bonanza?*

Inez looked like a lost puppy, fragile and helpless.

*I can't face her… I just can't… definitely not!* I took out my cell phone and dialed her number. She answered it on the first ring.

"Hello?" Inez's seductive voice said.

"Hi, sweetheart. I was calling because I miss you. What are you doing?"

"I'm at a meeting. I'll give you a call when I'm done, okay? Come over to my place tonight."

"I'll be there, baby."

"Okay, Ma, I'll call you soon. Love you!"

I knew going over to her crib was not a possibility. I had to get away. My relationship with Inez was history--done. It was time to move on by myself to bigger and better things.

I watched Inez for another half hour, wondering to myself how the fuck she would react if she ever found out that I was her biological mother. It didn't even matter. With great effort, I walked out of Cousin Food Market through the back exit, which led towards 5th Street. Once I reached 5th Street, I took one more look towards Isla Verde, and allowed my tears to freely roll down my face and into the gutter of North Philadelphia. Then I flagged down a cab.

"Where to?" the Haitian taxi driver asked.

"Market Street," I responded.

My head was spinning in circles. I wanted to write this

whole day off as a mistake. I was crushed. I still couldn't believe this shit. My mouth opened in a silent scream.

Once the taxi reached Market Street, I gave the cab drive a fifty-dollar bill and got out the car not waiting for my change. I wanted to run, but I could've run all day and still not be able to run from myself. I still would be a thirty-five year old woman who had just learned that she been sucking and fucking her long lost daughter's pussy. But damn, it was good!

Since it was still early, I went to Inez's apartment and taped the letter I had written to my daughter on her front door, sealed with the prints of my lips, and signed it "Mom".

I scanned through my bag until I found my cell phone, pulled it out and pressed the speed dial button. William picked up after the fourth ring.

"William, it's me, Mita. Have you thought about my offer about leaving with me?"

William took his time answering.

*I hope this clown don't start some bullshit.*

"I thought about it, and to be honest with you, boo, I decided to stay here. I mean, my whole family is here, my job... I mean, can we talk about this later? I'm busy right now."

*I know this nigga is not trying to brush me off as if I was some fucking whore from down the block!* "Nigga, are you serious?"

"Yeah, I'm serious. Plus, after thinking about it, how the fuck do I know I'm the father? Shit, you gave me the pussy like you were giving out Welfare cheese. If anything, I want a DNA test before I claim anybody's baby." William was acting like a bitch ass nigga, which demonstrated to me that he wasn't ready for this bitch on the move. I wasn't even mad at him. However, I did wonder about my next move.

"Nah, nigga, fuck you and a DNA test! You don't have to worry about me at all," I said. Just when I was about to cut him off, I heard a woman's over the phone voice say, "You ready to bust that nut in my face, daddy?" I smiled, because this nigga was getting his dick sucked while shining on me. *Now ain't that a bitch?* "Damn, William! You're really showing me your true colors. Shining on me while getting some head. I'll make sure to tell your child how you decided to bypass being a father for some head. You are just like every other nigga in the 'hood!" I threw my cell phone on the ground and stepped on it until it was in pieces.

*I got to get the fuck out this city!*

Inez's face kept forcing itself back into my consciousness. Her voice, her smile, her touch was like a brain tumor, consuming my whole existence a second at a time.

# CHAPTER 29
## "No Love Lost"

*What the fuck am I doing here waiting for some stranger? Fuck this shit!* My head started buzzing as my adrenaline surged. I slammed both palms down on the hood of my car with a flat smack. My nostrils were flared as I looked down American and Lehigh Avenue, hoping for a miracle. *Maybe she's running late. Nah! Fuck this shit! I don't have time for this shit! Maybe the world doesn't revolve around me.* Every letdown I suffered always stirred something within me. Anger. Jealousy. I was jealous because I felt alone in this cruel world. I had nobody to confide in.

The realization of me never locating my biological mother finally dawned on me. "Fuck it! Let nature take its course. I got to play the cards I've been dealt," I said out loud.

Not knowing what else to do, I got back into my car. I sat for a moment, feeling like I should be somewhere. But where?

I turned the radio on to Philly's number one radio station, Power 99, and instantly began singing along with the soulful voice of Mary J. Blige's "No More Drama", quickly forgetting about all the drama in my life. Mary J. Blige's songs always made me feel like a super woman.

Driving through 5$^{th}$ Street, *El Bloque De Oro* (The Golden Block), which is where a large potion of the Puerto Ricans live, brought back bad memories. Whether I like it or not, this was home to me. This is where I first got introduced to the cruel realities of life. This where I was forced to fend for myself when my foster father became addicted to my pudding. *At least I made something out of myself.* I know plenty of girls and boys who had fallen victim to the same society that raised me to be the cold bitch that I am. I can admit that I'm a damaged soul, but at least I know the reason why.

I parked in front of the Storage Center on Delaware Avenue. As I walked into the Storage Center, the rent-a-cop, an old black man, gave me a strange look, as if he wanted to say something to me but just couldn't muster up the balls to do so.

"Excuse me, young lady, but wasn't you here earlier today?" the old man asked, letting his glasses fall to the bridge of his nose.

"No!" I caught myself fighting back a surge of anger. I wanted to bitch slap that old bastard.

"No?"

"Old man, what part of 'no' don't you understand? The N or the O?"

"Young lady, I know I'm old, but I still have a good memory. I could swear I saw you here earlier today. Do you have a twin sister or a daughter or something? I know I'm not crazy," he said, looking at me with irritation in his eyes.

*I had a bad feeling about this. I stood there staring at the old man, wondering what should I do. Damn! Were the police on to me? Should I just walk out and take the loss? Maybe I'm overreacting. Maybe the old bastard is in fact crazy. This is probably nothing.* "This is probably a mistake." A few moments of silence invaded the space between the old man and me.

"No, I don't make mistakes. Follow me and I show you." He gripped my hand as if I was a little girl.

"Where we going?" I asked.

"I'm going to show you the security monitor so you won't think I'm crazy. Old man Billy Ray's been working this job for thirty years. I don't make mistakes."

Once we were behind the front desk counter, Billy Ray turned a small TV monitor towards me, then rewound the tape.

"Oh shit!" I said as I saw a familiar face on the monitor.

"Just a sec. You telling me that's not you?" Billy Ray asked, pointing at the monitor.

"No, that's not me!" My gut grew cold.

"I guess old man Billy Ray been on the job too long, huh?"

"I guess so."

When I stepped into my storage space, I felt my face flush with anger. I knew what was at stake here. I was beyond mad. *How can this bitch betray me like this?* Just by the way the boxes were tilted, I knew Sweet Lips had helped herself to my shit. The duffel bag I took from Solo was also missing. *Eso mi pasa por pendeja!* In my heart I knew Sweep Lips had signed her own Death Certificate.

"Damn! I can't believe this shit!" I lay in bed crying and asking God, "Why me?" No longer was I paying the reporter any mind. My full attention was now on the naked man being led to a police car by none other than Special Agent Jasmine Rodriguez. "Goddamnit!" I shouted.

The image of El Bodegero had me heading down Memory Lane, and there was nothing I could do now that would make a difference. Images of El Bodegero raping me flashed through my mind. For a second, I saw my mother sucking on the devil's dick, and Rafael choking the shit out of me. I saw Mrs. Penny face, and I felt her holding my hand while I gave birth. Then I saw my daughter's face for the first time. I felt a deep pain swirling throughout my body. My hands were trembling. "I can't live like this! I can't... I just can't!"

Nothing in my fucked up life could've prepared me for the bullshit that just dropped in my lap. As I sat in my car contemplating my next move, I could taste the bitterness rising in my throat. *I don't believe this whore played me!*

I tried calling Sweet Lips to see what bullshit excuse she would give me, but I got her voice mail. Next, I called my partner in crime, Cuba, the cleanup man also known as Ed Sanchez, a local ATF agent who specialized in ripping off drug dealers. I punched a few buttons on my cell phone and listened to it ring. A moment later, I heard Cuba's raspy voice.

"Hello?"

"Cuba."

"Speaking."

"It's me, Jasmine."

"I know who you are."

"We got problems."

"We? Bitch, since when we became friends?"

"This is serious, man!"

"I'm not playing! *You* got problems, not me," he said noncommittally.

"Are you going to hear me out?"

"What's the problem?"

"We need to move our stash from the storage center. I don't trust them people down there." I conveniently left out the fact that I was robbed by some dyke bitch who I'd fallen in love with.

"I don't like the sound of this."

"What part of this don't you like?"

"Moving our stash! You and I are the only ones who know about our stash, right? What's going on?"

"I can't explain over the phone. I just need you to help me clean this little mess up. Plus, I'ma pay you a quarter-mil at the end of the day." I took a deep breath.

"Does this mess call for someone to wind up with a toe tag?"

"I just need you for muscle. I can handle the rest. So, are you in or out?" I asked, feeling a little paranoid. When you've been an CIA agent long enough, you get a little paranoid.

"I'm in, only if you let me tap that fat ass of yours tonight."

"Cuba, I'm into the same thing you are into; pussy. But if I ever decide on going back to dick, you'll be the first to know about it, okay?" Sometimes a bitch gots to play with a nigga's ego, especially if you're trying to get him to do some dirty shit for you.

"I'll be waiting."

"Good! Meet me down at Melange."

"The Italian-Black restaurant in Cherry Hill?"

"Yes."

"Why so far? Why can't we meet down at Porky Points? You know I really don't fuck with Italian food. I'm Cuban, *mamita*. I eat rice and beans."

"I'll see you in a half hour." I ended the conversation because Cuba was longwinded, and for real for real, I wasn't in the mood for bullshit.

I looked at the phone in my hand and dialed Sweep Lips' number. Then I heard it ringing. Ten times... fifteen times... twenty times. My fucking heart pounded in my ribcage as the ringing continued. I knew that this bitch was still in town. I re-dialed Cuba's number again.

"Whassamatta?"

"You still in the office?"

"Yes. You said meet you in half."

"I know what I said. I need you to do me a quick favor. Run this name through AFIS and see what you can come up with."

"Name?"

"Mita Cruz."

"Why is this important? You know without fingerprints I may not come up with anything."

"Shut the fuck up! Just try. I'll see you in half," I said with a smile.

I pulled up in front of Melange in record time, fifteen minutes. The restaurant was small, so I selected a table directly across from the front door because I didn't want to have my back turned towards the door. I wasn't in the mood for eating.

Ten minutes later, Cuba walked in looking at his watch. "Damn, girl! How the fuck did you beat me down here?" he asked while rubbing his hand down my ass, copping himself a free feel.

"I'm always on time."

"So, what's so important that you made me drive down here? This shit better be good."

"Did you run that name through AFIS?"

"Yes, I did. She was easy to find because she was already in the system."

"What you got?"

"She was just recently released from prison. She has no investments, no obligations, parents are both dead. In fact, she murdered them. No siblings. She's an only child, just like you."

"You're insulting me, asshole!"

"Just joking, baby!"

"Cuba, seriously, is that all you got?"

"If you let me finish, I'll tell you what else I have."

"Speak."

"I also ran a quick check of the surrounding hotels, and someone by the name of Mita Cruz checked into the Marriott this afternoon."

"No way! She can't be that stupid!" I exhaled deeply through my nostrils.

"Apparently she is."

"Let's rock out!"

"Hold up! What about my food?"

"Are you serious?"

"Yeah, I'm serious! I'm hungry!"

"Cuba, you can eat later. I've got to track this bitch down before she tries to skip town with your quarter-mil." I knew this would take his mind off of food for a while.

"I'm hungry now!"

"Chill, nigga! Maybe I'll treat you to some of this *dessert*!" I said, rubbing my hand on the inside of his leg.

"I'ma hold you to that!" Cuba said, squeezing his hard on.

I decided that the best thing to do would be to do what I learned in prison; avoid and ignore. Lying in bed crying wasn't helping me. I got my ass off the bed and took a cold shower. I thought about calling Inez, but decided not to. I walked out of the room, looking only where I was going and not looking back. This hotel room held too many memories. This was the room Inez and I spent the night in the first time we got it on. I kept my focus forward even as I walked out the Marriott Hotel, refusing to even glance back at the place that held a piece of my soul.

# CHAPTER 30
## "Still Damaged"

I parked in the shadows on the opposite side of the Marriott Hotel. That offered me an unobstructed view of the front door. If someone walked in or out, I'd see them. I looked over at Cuba who had lust in his eyes, and winked at him. I knew that playing with his male ego would keep him in suspense.

After a while, I did notice a familiar face standing on the corner. Universal City never looked this beautiful. She stepped to the curb and hailed a cab.

"Ow! Shit!" I yelled as I opened the door to my car with my Glock 9 in my hand, ready to make Sweet Lips pay for her betrayal. But Cuba grabbed my hand.

"No, Wait! Not now!" he shouted.

"What?"

"Not now. Too many people out here. Plus, she's empty-handed. Let's just follow her." He nodded and exhaled a wet, gurgling breath.

I fixed my gaze on him. "Okay," I said.

"One step at a time. We've done well so far. We found her, so trust me, she'll lead us to the money," Cuba said, licking his lips while watching Sweet Lips.

*Men are easily distracted when they see a fine bitch with a fat ass.* "There!" I said pointing.

"I see it," Cuba said.

My patience was running out. The cab stopped in front of a Target store on Delaware Avenue. Within three minutes, Sweet Lips returned to the cab with a plastic bag in her hand. Cuba and I stared at her for a long moment, clearly trying to figure out what the fuck this disloyal bitch was doing.

Following the cab was a pain in the ass, because we had to stay at least six cars behind. I was furious, because I felt I wasting so much time following her.

Twenty minutes later, the cab arrived at the Cheltenham Cemetery. It was 8:30 p.m., and the Pennsylvania sky was already dark. Cuba and I watched her walk into the cemetery office. The groundskeeper smiled and reached for a handful of Sweet Lip's perfectly round ass.

"What the fuck is she doing?" I asked Cuba, hoping he could tell me something that could make my fingers stop trembling.

"It looks like she's trying to buy her way into the cemetery. How convenient is that for us?" Cuba asked a question that required no answer, because I definitely wanted to kill this bitch.

"Whoa! Take it easy! I got plans for this whore. She's got to pay for her dirty deeds."

"Uh-oh!" Cuba said.

We watched Sweet Lips kneel down by a gravesite, then pull out a portable shovel from the bag she was carrying in her hand. She started digging next to the headstone, pulling out what appeared to be two black duffel bags. *Damn! This bitch got game, burying money in the cemetery. I should'a thought about that myself.*

Cuba and I walked into the cemetery office where the groundskeeper was jerking off behind the counter. Immediately, Cuba snapped his neck, leaving him slumped over the counter with his dick in his hand. "Fuck him! He got the same treatment the Judge got," Cuba said to me as I slowly walked toward Sweep Lips.

"Sweet Lips!" I yelled. She glanced up at me. Cuba was on her ass like white on rice. She stood up, holding onto the two the duffel bags as if her life dependent on them. "Easy now, bitch!" I said to her.

Sweet Lips stared towards the cemetery office.

"Don't be stupid!"

She tried to run, but Cuba pimp slapped the shit out of her, knocking her ass to the ground.

"Help! Help! Help!" she screamed at the top of her lungs.

Cuba slammed her on top of Ms. Penny's gravesite.

"Bitch, ain't nothing but dead mothafuckas in here. You can scream all you want. Nobody gives a fuck about you," I said, slapping a pair of plastic restraint cuffs on her wrists and lifting her off of the ground by her hair.

"What did I do to you, baby?" Sweet Lips asked in a seductive tone.

"Bitch, play dumb if you want!" I said, crushing her right check with the butt of my Glock until it was dark purple and swollen.

Once Cuba threw the two duffel bags in the trunk of the car, he threw Sweet Lips in the back seat.

I had no doubt that they were going to kill me. Inez's eyes were burning a hole in my soul. After driving around for about a half hour, I thought they were going to take me to the middle of nowhere or maybe a stash house, but instead they took me to a warehouse near Penn's Landing. From the warehouse, I could see directly across the Delaware River into the River Front State Prison.

"Okay, bitch, get out of the car!" Cuba ordered me with a fist to my mouth, splitting my bottom lip in half.

I sobbed. Raw fear held me at a grip.

"You betrayed me. You stole my money. Now you must suffer the consequences. I'm going to teach you a lesson until you beg for death!" Inez said, popping the trunk of her car open, pulling out a blue duffel bag which contained what she considered her tools. The truth of my existence hovered nearby. Inez gave me a ready-to-rip-your-head-off look.

"What's done in the dark always comes to the light," Cuba muttered under his breath as he waited for Inez to dish out her next set of orders to him.

"Baby, I can explain it to you. It's not what you think it is. Please, let me explain it to you." I was hoping to touch a soft spot in her.

"Cuba, strip this whore naked."

Cuba commenced to strip and tie me up, taping my ankles together. The sight of my hairless pussy had Cuba on it.

"Baby, please! You've got to believe me! I wasn't trying to burn you for your money. I just couldn't face you after I found out that I--"

"Shut the fuck up, bitch! As a matter of fact, stuff her mouth with her panties. I'm not trying to hear shit."

I couldn't believe she wouldn't let me speak. Even with my mouth taped up with my panties in it, I kept speaking, trying to tell her that I was her mother, but it was fruitless.

Teardrops cascaded from my eyes as Cuba bent me over a table and parted my ass cheeks apart and rammed his large dick up my ass without lubrication. With every stroke I felt my insides being torn apart. My asshole felt as if it was on fire. I screamed beyond the tape for him to stop, but every effort I made seemed to excite him more. The more I screamed, the deeper he went. He plunged his long dick into the depths of my core.

"You see, bitch, this is just the beginning. I got a whole lot more in store for your ass!" Inez whispered in my ear as she removed my panties from my mouth, which were covered with blood and my own saliva.

"I'm your mother, Inez!" I yelled the second the panties landed on the floor.

"You got jokes, huh? If you think you're gonna suddenly be Mother of the Year, you're too late!"

"Inez, listen to me! I'm the person you were supposed to meet today. I was there. I saw you when you arrived in your car.

Remember, I called? You have to believe me!"

*What if this whore is telling the truth? Nah! She's just trying to buy some time on her life. I got to stick to my original plans. She's gotta die.* "I don't have a mother! My mother is dead! I'm adopted!"

"No! No! No! Baby, you have a mother and a father. I know you were adopted. But I'm your mother!"

"Show me the truth in black and white!"

"I can't at this point, but it's the truth." Pain and grief were etched in my face. I wasn't ready to die. I couldn't think of what to say, so I decided to share with her that I was pregnant. Maybe she'd have a little compassion for me. "Inez, I'm pregnant!"

"Pregnant! So you been double dipping behind my back too, bitch?"

*Maybe telling her I was pregnant, was a mistake!*

Inez tightened her hand on my hair. She yanked my head back so hard that my neck snapped from the force. "Open your fucking mouth! Cuba, hold her mouth open."

Cuba placed his hand on my jaw and gripped tight, forcing my mouth open. Inez than took a bottle out of her tool bag, untwisted the top and forced some kind of clear liquid down my throat. At first I thought it was water, then I literally felt my unborn child burning inside my stomach. My body began to tremble, and my vision became blurry. I couldn't breathe. I looked at Inez for the last time and managed to croak out, "I... I... I... I... love you!"

"Flip her over, Cuba!" I didn't want to leave any evidence that could be linked to me, so I decided to clean Cuba's mess up. I inserted the nozzle of the bottle into Sweet Lips' busted asshole and poured the rest of the liquid, up her ass.

"You are one sick bitch! What the fuck was that?"

"Acid!"

We both looked at Sweet Lips' body lying on the floor with her eyes open.

"Is she dead?" Cuba asked.

"She looks dead to me."

"Now, baby girl, let's talk business. Them two duffel bags in the trunk look like they contain more then a quarter of a mil," Cuba said while looking down at Sweet Lips' body.

*I must admit, even dead the bitch had a special kind of sex appeal.* "Cuba, why do you always want to get greedy with me? Don't I always take care of you? Don't I always keep your pockets fat? Don't I always pay your gambling debts? This ain't about no money. You can have both duffel bags, only because I appreciate you as a partner. But stop being greedy. A greedy mothafucka always ends up hungry again. Now, clean this mess up. Do what you do best." I gave him a wink as I rubbed my own ass, then added, "I hope you got some more energy left, because today is your lucky day. I want some of that big Cuban dick. I hope you're ready for some dyke pussy." I knew that the job would not be complete until Sweet Lips' body was wrapped up in plastic bags and disposed of in the gutter of North Philadelphia.

In the pet cemetery down Germantown and Indiana

Avenue, Cuba and I dropped Sweet Lips' abused corpse.

"Baby girl, I can't believe there's two-mil in each bag! I could definitely use some of that money to pay of some of my bills."

"As said before, stop acting greedy with me."

"Baby girl, you know I got love for you. So, are you going to let me hit the pussy tonight?"

"Yes."

Cuba nodded his head. When he knelt down to cut the ATF issued plastic cuffs off of Sweet Lips' wrists, I eased my Glock out and placed it on the back of his head. Cuba's eyes blink for a second, but it was too late. I squeezed the trigger, blessing his greedy ass with nine hot hollow tipped bullets to the back of his head. The front of his face was completely blown off.

As a trained assassin for the government, I had been trained to never leave any evidence that could one day be used against me, even if it meant killing a co-worker. Cuba knew too much, and had enough dirt on me to blackmail me or put me away for life in prison, and with his greedy tendencies, I knew it wouldn't be long before he would try to blackmail me. Fuck him! He got what he deserved!

When I arrived back at my apartment, I instantly recognized Sweet Lips' lip prints on a note taped to my door. A smile came over my face, because she took with her a piece of my soul. I will admit, the bitch had me pussy whipped, but a bitch got to do what she has to do. I took the note and tucked it in my pocket. I wanted to read it after I took a warm shower and lay between my

Egyptian cotton sheets.

I almost came on myself while taking a shower thinking of Sweet Lips. *Damn! Why did she play herself like that?*

A half hour later I lay in my bed butt ass naked, and decided to read the note Sweet Lips had left me. I opened the note and began reading it:

> *Dear Inez:*
>
> *I know you are probably mad at me for not doing this in person, but I just can't. I can't bear to look at you again. Remember when we first met that I was looking for my daughter? Well I found her today. Inez, you are the daughter I've been looking for. Maybe one day we will sit down and talk face to face. I know you have many questions, and hopefully I can provide you with some answers. At this moment, I need time to heal. Your father's name is Gilberto "El Bodegero" Colon, and you can locate him at the Federal Detention Center in downtown Philadelphia.*
>
> *I will always love you, my child!*
> *Love always,*
> *Mita "Sweet Lips" Cruz*

By the time I was done reading Sweet Lips' note, tears began to roll down my face. *Damn! She was telling me the truth! Nah! This gotta be a big joke! I know I just didn't kill my biological mother! Nah, I know game when I see it. Why does the name Gilberto "El Bodegero" Colon sound so familiar? Hell no!* I picked up my cell phone and placed a call to the CIA building.

"Hello, Agent Santos speaking."

"Sam, It's me, Jasmine. I have a quick question. What's the full name of the suspect we arrested this morning?"

"Gilberto Colon. I was just about to call you. Our suspect was found hanging in his cell about a half hour ago. I guess this case is closed."

"Thank you for letting me know." I shut my eyes and let his words penetrate my already damaged soul.

**One Week Later**...

"Ms. Rodriguez, I believe I found a perfect match for you. Now, it may cost you an extra hundred thousand, but I can assure you that you will be number one on the list," Doctor Miller said with a smile.

"No problem. But when will I be able to get the transplant?"

"Ms. Rodriguez, I can have you in and out of the hospital in less than two weeks. As stated, I have the perfect match. Almost as if it was tailor made for you."

"One more question. Whose kidney am I about to get?"

"Some raped murder victim. My brother, who works at the Medical Examiner's office, made the match. Nobody will ever know. The body was never claimed. As a matter of fact, here, look at the victim."

Doctor Miller pushed a photograph taken by the Medical Examiner and placed it in front of me.

"She probably was a crackhead, but she had good kidneys. Lucky for you, huh?" he said with a smile.

I just stared at the picture in disbelief.

As I walked out of the doctor's office, a young Latina drove by me in a dark blue, beat up van with the radio on blast playing the soulful duo of father and son, Eddie and Gerald Levert. The words to the song slapped me in the face:

*"...Girl, you know there ain't nothing I wouldn't do for you,*
*And baby don't... don't ever doubt my love, 'cause is truth for*
*you.*

*Baby, hold on to me, see I'm the special kind..."*

Sweet Lips' face flashed into my mind, because the last words she said to me were, *"I love you!"*

People always said that the truth is stranger than fiction.

# ABOUT THE AUTHOR

David Gonzalez, a.k.a. LSD Gonzalez, was born in the South Bronx. In the early 8O's, he became associated with the notorious South Bronx street gang, The Pop Rulers. After being implicated in several crimes in three different states, and after being found NOT GUILTY, he was transferred to Pennsylvania, where he is currently fighting his prison sentence.

LSD is also an international award-wining artist. He's been featured in several national documentaries, such as "Red Clay Country", Steel, Concrete and Paint", and is the recipient of the international Cindy Gold, Aurora Award, and World-fest Platinum Award for the U.S. international film, "Prison Dialogue: Message to the Youth" documentary.

He has written serial articles on prison life, three novels, and holds a degree in general education from Villanova University.

He had served time in Lewisburgh, Atlanta, Texarkana, and Leavenworth Federal Penitentiary. He currently resides in the fifth largest state prison in the United States, Gaterford.

NEW VISION PUBLICATION PRESENTS
Available Everywhere!!!!
Tit 4 Tat
A NOVEL BY
ALONZO L. STR
Payback's A
Tit4Tat Part 3
Coming Soon!
NEW VISION PUBLICATION PRESENTS
Tit 4 Tat
Payback's A Bitch
Part 2
A NOVEL BY
ALONZO L. STRANGE
ALONZO L. STRANGE